WE ARE STILL
TORNADOES

WE ARE STILL TORNADOES

MICHAEL KUN *and* SUSAN MULLEN

ST. MARTIN'S GRIFFIN

NEW YORK

From Susan

For my husband, Kevin, and our daughters, Hannah and Haley

From Michael

For my wife, Amy, and our daughter, Paige

WE ARE STILL TORNADOES. Copyright © 2016 by Michael Kun and Susan Mullen. All rights reserved. Printed in the United States of America. For information, address St. Martin's Press, 175 Fifth Avenue, New York, N.Y. 10010.

www.stmartins.com

Designed by Omar Chapa

Library of Congress Cataloging-in-Publication Data

Names: Kun, Michael, author. | Mullen, Susan, author.
Title: We are still tornadoes / Michael Kun and Susan Mullen.
Description: First edition. | New York : St. Martin's Griffin, 2016.
Identifiers: LCCN 2016010640| ISBN 9781250098405 (hardcover) |
  ISBN 9781250098412 (ebook)
Subjects: LCSH: Man-woman relationships—Fiction. | Mate selection—
  Fiction. | Friendship—Fiction. | First loves—Fiction. | BISAC: JUVENILE
  FICTION / Love & Romance. | JUVENILE FICTION /Family / General
  (see also headings under Social Issues). | JUVENILE FICTION / Social
  Issues / Dating & Sex. | GSAFD: Bildungsromans. | Love stories.
Classification: LCC PS3561.U446 W4 2016 | DDC 813/.54—dc23
LC record available at https://lccn.loc.gov/2016010640

Our books may be purchased in bulk for promotional, educational, or business use. Please contact your local bookseller or the Macmillan Corporate and Premium Sales Department at 1-800-221-7945, extension 5442, or by e-mail at MacmillanSpecial Markets@macmillan.com.

First Edition: November 2016

10 9 8 7 6 5 4 3 2

1982
AUGUST

Dear Cath,

Good luck in college!
Thanks for four years of English homework.
See you at Thanksgiving!

Scott

P.S. Nice underwear!

Dearest Scott,

Thank you so much for the heartwarming note that you so kindly
placed in my suitcase. I can't tell you how much it meant to me to
arrive in my dorm room on my first day of college, filled with both
excitement and anxiety, only to discover your note in my suitcase
among my underwear which, oddly, were no longer folded in the
same manner that I had folded them before I shut my suitcase.

College is overwhelming so far. Absolutely, incredibly, unbelievably overwhelming. The campus itself is twice the size of East
Bloomfield, and there's not a person here who isn't wearing a T-shirt or
a baseball cap that says WAKE FOREST on it, as if we might forget what
college we're going to. (Like this stationery my dad bought me at the
school store *minutes* after we'd unloaded the car! How do you like it?
Does it help you remember where I'm going to school?) There are lots
of very nice people—everyone's always smiling and saying "Hey!"
around here!—but it's absolutely, incredibly, unbelievably overwhelming. Fortunately, all the other freshmen are in the same boat, except
they probably didn't have someone going through their underwear.

Anyway, classes don't even start for three days. Maybe I won't
feel so overwhelmed by then. And maybe everyone will stop smiling then, too.

By the way, it's very odd sleeping in a room with a complete
stranger. (Please insert your own lame sex joke here.) My roommate's name is Mary Baird Dorothy Something-or-other, but

4

thankfully she said we can call her "Dorothy" for short. She seems very sweet so far, but maybe too sweet, if you know what I mean. Like cotton candy. (That's called a simile, which you would know if you'd been paying attention in English.) Dorothy has a poster tacked up over her bed of a cat hanging from a tree branch. In big red letters, it says HANG IN THERE, BABY! It doesn't quite go with my Elvis Costello poster. Maybe my tastes will match up better with some of the other girls on my hall. I've met about a dozen or so already. I can't tell you any of their names. Thank God for name tags!

Here's the other thing: Don't tell my parents, but I have to admit that I'm a little homesick already. There, I said it. And I will deny saying it until my dying days. But I've never been away from home before, and it's so strange not to have my mom and dad right down the hall if I need anything. I especially miss Plum. I hope my mom remembers to feed her. I know my dad won't.

Please write back soon, okay? And please, please, stay away from my underwear! A girl's undergarments are a private matter, my friend. (Sorry, but I'm still not going to say "panties." You know that word gives me the creeps. Like "moist." I shivered just writing that.)

Love,
Catherine

P.S. Did I mention that Dorothy's a snorer? It sounds like someone's operating heavy machinery five feet away from me. I just hope I can hang in there, baby.

P.P.S. What happened to you last week? You disappeared on me. I can't believe we didn't get a chance to say good-bye.

P.P.P.S. Tell your parents I said hi. And that you're a perv.

SEPTEMBER

September 2, 1982

Dear Cath,

I'm appauled that you would accuse me of going through your panties when I left that heartwarming note in your suitcase. Appauled, I tell you. (Did I spell "appauled" correctly? If not, please correct it for me.) Just so we're clear, are you talking about the yellow bikini ones with the stars on the hip that were packed right beneath your running shoes? Or the light blue bikini ones with the white polka dots? Or the hot pink ones? Or the orange-and-red ones? Or that really big beige pair that you must have stolen from your grandmother?

Seriously, though, your stupid dog knocked over the entire suitcase when I was trying to stick the note inside. I had to scramble to put everything back into the suitcase. And that's the story I'll tell the police!

Anyway, unless your roommate hung it up to be funny, the HANG IN THERE, BABY poster is pretty scary. Didn't Mrs. Wilkins have that same stupid poster behind her desk in fourth grade? But your Elvis Costello poster's even scarier, if you ask me. You'd never even *heard* of Elvis Costello until I got you to listen to him over the summer, and now you have his poster up on your wall to try to convince everyone that you're the cool chick in the dorm? How sad. How very, very sad. You better pray I don't come down to visit you in whatever state Wake Forest is in and tell all your new buddies about how you were still listening to Tony Orlando and Dawn just a few months ago. Yes, you'd better get on your knees and pray, college girl.

On a different note, my job is terrible. The days are endless. That's what I get for working at my father's store, I suppose. Yes, I know, it's my own damn fault. If I'd just "buckled down" and "put my nose to the grindstone" and gotten some decent "grades," I could have gone off to college like you and everyone else in our class, but I "didn't" do those things, and it's too late to "cry over spilled milk." I "made my bed," and now I have to "lie" in it. I imagine I'll work at "Agee's Men's Clothing" until it becomes "Agee & Son's Men's Clothing." Then someday my father will die—it's going to be a heart attack, in case you want to bet—and it will become "Agee's Men's Clothing" again. I will have spent my whole life selling clothes to people in this "one-horse town," and I will be "fat" and "old" and "disgusting." But your mother will still have a crush on me.

I think I use quotation marks too much. What do you "think," college girl?

And I really do think your mother has a crush on me. (By the way, I saw her walking Plum last night. I assume she's feeding her, too.)

Oh, did I mention that Samantha broke up with me? I know I didn't mention it, but I waited a few paragraphs to tell you to make it sound casual. Did it work? Anyway, after we agreed that we would date long-distance while she was at college,

9

she sent me a letter telling me she'd met someone else at school and didn't think it would be fair to lead me on. She sent me the letter after her *third* day at college. Three days, can you believe it? Honestly, I'm more surprised than hurt. I figured we could stick it out until Christmas, at the very least. But three days? I've had pimples that have lasted longer than that. I've had gas that's lasted longer than that. You get the point.

I have to go do something very important right now, at least as far as you know. Hope you're having fun at school, college girl.

Scott

P.S. Did I tell you that my dad is giving me a 10% discount off anything at the store? How cool is that? (I'm being serious. I really want to know how cool that is. I think the answer is, "Not very," but I'm not sure.)

P.P.S. Want me to send you some Tony Orlando and Dawn albums to listen to when you get homesick?

P.P.P.S. Three days! Can you believe it?

My Dearest Scottie,

I knew Plum knocked over the suitcase. I asked my mom how you left me a note in my suitcase since my dad made you give back the key to our house after that party, and she said she let you go up to my bedroom, but she heard Plum knock over the suitcase and heard you cursing a blue streak. So you're off the hook. For now.

And I'll deal with the dorm room poster thing in a minute.

But first, if you're going to insist on calling me "college girl," then I'm going to start calling you "underachiever guy." Or "really bad speller boy." How does that work for you? (By the way, it's "appalled.")

And yes, you do overuse quotation marks. Particularly since you also misuse quotation marks. Who puts "grades" in quotation marks? Oh, yeah—you do. Which is why I had to "help you" through "English class" all during "high school," underachiever guy.

I'm sorry work sucks, but I love your dad's store! I love everything about it. I really do, although I've never been there for eight hours at a time. Maybe it will get more interesting when it gets busier for the holidays. Or maybe you'll move up and get more involved in other aspects of the business. (There are other aspects, right?) I don't know, but your dad always seems happy and that's where he's worked forever, so it can't be *that* bad, right? (I have some very fond memories of coming into the store to see you, and your dad calling me his "little Catherine" and sneaking me some hard candies.

Speaking of which, you might want to check under that last suit rack in the back corner. I never really liked the orange ones.) Or maybe you'll change your mind and go to college. Despite your quotation mark "challenges," and despite your spelling challenges, you are way smarter than most of the people here. Besides me, of course.

You think my mom has a crush on you? Please. My mother is thrilled that you will eat her cooking. My dad and I know better. And yelling the F-word (as my mom would say) at Plum when she knocked over my suitcase didn't endear you to my mother at all, trust me. Although I have to admit that I enjoyed making her repeat it over the phone.

As for your news about Samantha, because you waited until the end of your letter before telling me about her, I've delayed in responding. That's called tit for tat. (Insert a lame sex joke here.) Samantha, Samantha, Samantha. What to say about Sa-Man-Tha? Um, okay. This is what I'm going to say about Samantha. Nothing. And do you know why? Because by the time you get this, Samantha may have come crawling back to you. Hopefully, literally crawling 200 miles on those bony little knees of hers from the Western Kentucky College for Morons, or whatever the name is of that "college" she's attending. My roommate, who's hanging in there, keeps saying, "This is just like camp! This is just like camp!" I'm guessing that she means that this whole college thing doesn't seem real. So maybe that's what Samantha's going through. Maybe she'll wake up and not be hungover for once in her life and realize what a huge mistake she's made. That you're the best thing that's ever happened to her. That she was lucky to have you. And that, really, she didn't deserve a minute of your time. But until I know that this really is a "breakup" and not just one of her Boone's Farm–fueled, bubble-headed freak-outs, I'll keep my opinions to myself.

Okay, on to the dorm room poster thing. Yes, I know you are Mr. Cool Music Guy and got Elvis's *My Aim Is True* before anybody else in the galaxy except for Elvis himself and maybe his mother, but I had to put *something* on my side of the room. Dorothy's mom showed up with matching black-and-gold Wake Forest bedspreads, curtains, and bulletin boards for *both* of us. I kid you not. I'd never even met them before, and they're going to pick out my bedspread? I said something like, "Well, gee, thanks, but I brought *my own* stuff." Her mom was clearly miffed and started banging nails into the walls and hanging up all these framed posters all over the place. Elvis is all I had, and I was sort of glad that it clashed with all their matchy-matchy stuff. Besides, "Accidents Will Happen" is like a theme song here. I've never seen so many people throw up! In bushes, in hallways, sometimes they even make it to the bathroom. It's disgusting. And then I hum "Accidents will happen . . . " and think about riding around town with you, listening to it on the tape deck, and then it's not so bad.

I have to go to the library. Classes started and there's a lot to do. They don't call this place "Work Forest" for nothing. And I have to tell you about my Calculus professor. My parents would die if they knew they were cutting a big check to Wake Forest to pay for this dork. He reminds me of Mr. Laire. Which isn't a compliment.

Write soon and let me know if Samantha is as dumb as I think she is. About the breakup, I mean.

Love,
College Girl

P.S. No, I don't want to bet on how your father will die! What is wrong with you?

P.P.S. Your dad's 10% discount? Not very cool. He used to give me 20% just for being so darned lovable.

P.P.P.S. Tony Orlando and Dawn are awesome, and "Knock Three Times" is super awesome. Don't pretend I was the only one who would dance to that song. I may even have pictures of you dancing to it that I could use as evidence.

September 9, 1982

Dear College Girl,

You have pictures that would prove I was dancing to a particular song? Tell me how that works exactly. How can you look at a picture and tell what song someone was dancing to? I mean, unless I am holding a sign that says, I'M DANCING TO A TONY ORLANDO AND DAWN SONG AT THE MOMENT THIS PICTURE IS BEING TAKEN, I don't see how that would work. Do you have a picture of me holding up a sign like that?

And please don't think I'm over here crying my eyes out over Samantha with the bony knees. (FYI—I didn't date her for her knees, if you know what I mean. I dated her for two other reasons. I'm trying to be subtle here. How am I doing at that?) I mean, if I had a dollar for every time I wanted to break up with her myself, I'd have a good six or seven dollars! Those are big bucks, my friend. The bigger problem is that there's no one left in town for me to date, now that everyone in our class is off at college. The only girls left are in high school, and I always thought it was creepy when guys graduated but still hung around the school afterwards. (Yes, I am referring to Todd Wilkerson. Remember how he came back and dated that crazy girl in our class after he had graduated? Oh, that's right, that was *you*, wasn't it? How could that have slipped my mind?) Anyway, I'm committed to not being one of those losers. (I'm committed to be an entirely different kind of loser!) But with

15

everyone gone, that pretty much reduces my potential dating pool to one person—your mom! Boy, will that be uncomfortable for you when you come home for Thanksgiving!

Speaking of high school, you'll never guess who came into the store looking for jeans yesterday. (Technically, he asked for "dungarees," not "jeans." Which is not only sad, but an appropriate use of quotation marks, too.) Mr. Mennori. Give me a D in Biology, then show up at my dad's store and ask for "dungarees" like it never happened? What a jerk. The funny thing is that for the first time in my life, I could say anything I wanted to him because he doesn't have any power over me anymore. He's just another tubby guy coming into the store and lying about the size of his waist. But instead of telling him to go screw himself, I shook his hand and actually said, "Nice to see you, Mr. Mennori." Can you believe it? "Nice to see you, Mr. Mennori"? I completely wimped out. Next time he comes in, I'm going to say something absolutely devastating that will make him wish he'd never crossed paths with me. I haven't thought of it yet, but I will. Mark my words. And whatever it is, it will be something your mother would be too embarrassed to repeat to you over the phone. (Did she really say "fuck"? I can't even imagine her saying that!)

College sounds terrific so far, college girl. Studying and vomiting. Sounds like I'm missing out on so much! In fact, tonight I may try to replicate the college experience by reading one of my old book reports with my finger down my throat.

Give Dorothy my love.

Your future stepfather,
Scott

P.S. Would it be too mean if I said something about that giant mushroom-looking thing on Mr. Mennori's elbow the next time he came in? (I'll answer my own question: Yes. But I'll bet you won't be able to eat mushrooms for a week now that I've got you thinking about it!)

P.P.S. In case you really have lost your sense of humor, college girl, I'm joking about marrying your mom. She's not even the most attractive woman in your family. No, that aunt of yours who came to your pool party was smoking hot! Can you send me her phone number? Do you have a picture of her dancing to a Tony Orlando and Dawn song?

P.P.P.S. I made you a tape of a great album by a British band called ABC. The album's called *The Lexicon of Love*. (I had to look up what "lexicon" means.) Every single song is a master-piece of pop music. "Poison Arrow" is my favorite, but "Look of Love" and "Tears Are Not Enough" are also incredible.

P.P.P.P.S. Calling me "underachiever guy"—is that supposed to be an insult or a compliment?

P.P.P.P.P.S. One more thing. I have a very important question to ask you, and I think you need to be sitting down when I ask it. Are you sitting down now? Okay, here it is: Are you still a Tornado?

Dear Scott,

Oh my God, I have NEVER laughed so hard in my life! Ever! And, to make it worse, I made the mistake of reading your letter during Biology class. I burst out laughing, and the professor froze as he was writing on the board and turned around to ask me if there was something I would like to share with the class. Seriously, like when we were in second grade and got busted passing notes. I couldn't imagine trying to explain it to an entire lecture hall, so I just apologized and tried not to actually, literally, physically die of embarrassment right then and there.

I tried to explain it to Dorothy later, but I must not have done a very good job of impersonating Donnie Dibsie giving his graduation speech, because Dorothy didn't get it at all. But, to answer your questions, YES, YES, A THOUSAND TIMES YES! I AM STILL A TORNADO! I WILL ALWAYS BE A TORNADO UNTIL THE DAY I DIE! (Which luckily was *not* this morning in Biology class.)

Okay, now that I've stopped laughing, the ABC tape is awesome. And the "underachiever guy" thing is a compliment, as far as you know. It means you're super smart, but you don't apply yourself.

I'm glad that you're not too torn up about dear, sweet Samantha, who, as we both know, is not the least bit dear or sweet. Oh God, I can't believe I just wrote that. Please, please don't reply with some gross joke about Samantha's sweetness. I swear I will not let you visit if you make a gross joke about *that*! (And, yes, everyone can clearly

19

see the two biggest reasons you dated her. Subtlety isn't your strong suit. And wearing bras isn't hers.)

Ugh. Anyway, while we are on the topic of losers, Todd Wilkerson was absolutely *not* a loser when I started dating him. How was I supposed to know that he'd go from being the coolest guy in the senior class to working at the gas station? Okay, so maybe it took me too long to figure out that he wasn't the strong, silent type and that he was just sort of, well, the dumb, silent type. But who wouldn't be blinded by that smile? And the flowing black hair. And the way his T-shirts hung off those shoulders. And, well, you get the point. So, I get it that you're worried about looking like a loser if you date a high school girl. How about the girls at the community college? Or driving down to Baltimore to meet some girls down there? Or what about trying some sort of coed sports thing, like softball or bowling? Okay, whatever, those aren't great ideas. I don't really know what to suggest, except maybe to reconsider the whole college thing?

I'm sorry if I gave you a bad impression of college with the vomiting stories. I guess not all 18-year-olds are as used to drinking as you and I are, probably because they came from towns where there were other things for kids to do after school. But there are guys here who can't even handle three beers. Puh-lease. But I really do like it here. I mean, I am homesick at times and I miss my parents and Plum, but most of the time, I really like it. Some people keep to themselves or are just annoying, but most people are open and really want to make friends and have fun. I'm becoming friends with people I wouldn't have hung out with in high school. Like this girl who lives in the triple next door to me, Jane, from Kansas City. She was a cheerleader and a drama person in high school, and she's kind of loud. She seems spacy and almost silly sometimes, but then in English Composition, she cranked out a paper about *Invisible Man* that was better than anything I could do (and of course, I obsessed about highlighting the novel and writing notes in the margins and rereading critical passages), and she tested into a second-year calculus class, which is just crazy. And she loves new music. She's been playing this great new record by a guy named Peter Gabriel that has a fantastic song on it called "Shock the Monkey." You'd like it. And we went to see this band that she told me about called R.E.M. The lead singer was wild! He was hitting himself on the head and dancing so crazily that I was seriously worried about him the whole time. Their music was awesome. You should definitely see them if they come to town. (And don't pretend you don't know where Wake Forest is. It's the town and state you write on the envelopes to your letters.)

We went to our first home football game last weekend with a big group from our dorm. People here actually get dressed up for football games. Does Agee's Men's Clothing even carry seersucker suits? Lots of older boys and alumni were wearing them, along with bow ties and shoes they call "bucks." And apparently I will need to figure out where to buy flowery sundresses down here before the next home game. I did NOT fit in at all with my T-shirt and jean shorts. It was so fun, though—sunny and gorgeous and kind of goofy to be singing the fight song and chanting along with the cheerleaders. Plus, everyone started drinking around 10 in the morning, which meant the lightweights were vomiting by noon.

Oops, another vomiting story. Sorry.

School itself isn't too bad. I'm retaking Calculus 1, so that's easy, and Mrs. Oberlin did a good job teaching us how to write a paper, so English Comp is okay. I had to drop out of French, though. In certain ways I'm realizing that our high school wasn't as great as our parents think it is, and I am certainly not ready to read French literature. I mean, I can read Flaubert in English, but not *in French*. The shocking thing, though, is that a lot of freshmen can! The kids who went to fancy private schools or boarding schools, man, they're fluent in multiple languages and have read everything already! I thought boarding schools were for screwed-up kids. Turns out, they are like mini colleges. The boarding school kids are pretty intimidating. They smoke clove cigarettes and wear scarves, if that tells you anything. It's hard to describe, but I probably won't be hanging out with them anytime soon.

Oh yeah, and Mr. Mennori. I've discovered that he was a horrible teacher. I'm thinking of majoring in Psych and doing a Pre-Med course load, so I'm also retaking Biology, which I think I've mentioned before. I thought it would be easy because we took it in high school, but I don't remember any of it. Which, by the way, does not mean that you can or should be rude to him the next time he comes into your store! You have to uphold the Agee family tradition of being super nice to your customers. Perhaps offering him a hard candy will put you in the correct frame of mind? You don't want to get fired and have to work at the gas station, like someone else we know.

Gotta run, but please give your mom and dad hugs for me and tell your mom that I miss her oatmeal raisin cookies! I tried one in the cafeteria here yesterday and almost broke my tooth. Which is my way of saying that your mom should feel free to send me a tin of her oatmeal raisin cookies!

Much love,
Catherine

P.S. No, my mom didn't actually say "fuck." She said, "He used the F-word, very loudly." She had to add in the "very loudly" part because for some reason she whispers when she says "the F-word," even though Plum is the only one around to hear her most of the time. But enough jokes about my mom, already! My dad would kill you if he found out you were talking about her that way. Okay, maybe not kill you, but he'd do whatever accountants do when someone's being disrespectful to their wives. Maybe throw his Texas Instruments calculator at you. The big one.

P.P.S. Speaking of my dad, did I mention that he has started calling me his "little princess" again whenever I call home, like he used to when I was eight or nine? He seems weird when I speak to him. And my mom sounds weird, too, but an entirely different kind of weird. Maybe I'm just not used to talking to them over the phone.

Have you seen them? Do they seem weird to you? Are they feeding Plum?

P.P.P.S. Jane just told me that a band called the English Beat is coming to play at Wake Chapel the second Saturday in October. Do you want to come visit and go see them with us? Let me know and I'll get an extra ticket. I think you'd really like it here. Everything but Dorothy. You're going to hate her with a capital *H* when you meet her. Trust me.

P.P.P.P.S. One more thing. Are you still a Tornado?

September 15, 1982

Dear College Girl aka Little Princess,

Damn straight I'm still a Tornado! I will be until the day I die!
And when I get to heaven and St. Peter asks me who I am, I'll
say, "I'm Scott Agee, and I AM A TORNADO!" I haven't figured
out how to say it in all capital letters, but I will. And then he
will direct me to that special place in heaven that's reserved for
Tornadoes.

And while we may both be Tornadoes, one of us has actually heard of Peter Gabriel, R.E.M., and the English Beat. I
swear, I really should come to visit just to rip the Elvis Costello
poster from your wall. You don't deserve it. (By the way, Peter
Gabriel used to be in Genesis. That's the band that did that song
called "The Lamb Lies Down on Broadway" that you liked.
And R.E.M.'s lead singer has curly hair and you can't understand a word he's saying, right? His name is Michael Stipe. It's
just a matter of time before they replace him with someone
who can e-nun-ci-ate. And the English Beat's lead singer is
named Dave Wakeling, in case you were wondering. Their best
song is called "Mirror in the Bathroom." I've played it for you
before: "Mirror in the bathroom / Please talk free / The door is
locked / Just you and me." Does that sound familiar?)

Speaking of coming to visit, I'd love to come down to see
the English Beat in October—and tell you all about them—but
I usually work on Saturdays. If you recall, that's the busiest day

25

of the week for Agee's Men's Clothing, "Where Men and Boys Have Shopped Since 1966." I'll see if I can convince my dad to let me leave work early, even if the men and boys are still shopping. I don't think he'd let me leave early to go see a band, though, so I'll probably tell him that you need me to drive down to whatever state your college is in so I can help you with something. It'll either be that you need help with calculus or that you're pregnant. Given that he's seen my math grades over the years, the pregnancy story would be more believable. And he might even give me some money to take you out to a nice dinner or something. (If that happens, I'll make sure to ask for extra money because you're eating for two.)

Now, as for your last letter, I need to be honest—I skipped all the paragraphs dealing with our old teachers or the classes you're taking. I'm sorry, but if I had any interest in school, I wouldn't be helping men and boys shop, would I? I assume you're doing great in all your classes, so thumbs-up for that. And I assume you think our old teachers suck, so another thumbs-up.

As for whether your parents are being weird, I don't know how to answer that. The only time I ever see your mom is when she forgets to close the shade in the bathroom when she's taking a shower, and even then it's only if I feel like walking all the way over to my closet to get the binoculars, take them out of the box, walk back to the window, etc. It's a whole production. Anyway, I'm sure she's fine. She probably just misses you since she's now stuck at home with your dad and your ugly dog. Or she's heard about your pregnancy. The news is spreading like wildfire, I tell you!

As for your dad, he's always been weird in my book. The only time I ever see him is when he's walking from his car to the front door when he gets home. He did come in the store for a new pair of pants, but I didn't help him. My dad did.

One more thing: so if you think Todd Wilkerson is such a loser because he didn't go off to college and got a job at a gas station instead, what does that say about me? And don't try to draw a distinction between a gas station and a clothing store. If my dad owned a gas station, I'd be working at a gas station—and you know it.

There, I've just made myself depressed. Looking forward to seeing how you're going to talk your way around this one, Ms. Psych Major. (Okay, I did read the paragraphs about your classes, but that doesn't mean they didn't bore the proverbial crap out of me. And, no, I don't recall which proverb that comes from.)

Scott

P.S. If your friend likes Peter Gabriel, tell her to check out the new album by Simple Minds called *New Gold Dream*. It just came out the other day, and it's phenomenal. The first song is called "Someone Somewhere in Summertime." It's really good. So is "Promised You a Miracle."

P.P.S. I know you're not a huge baseball fan, but have you seen what the Orioles are doing? They're making a last-minute run to make the play-offs, and it's incredible! We've been watching them on TV or listening on the radio almost every night. I think they can do it. They've got a great young team. Eddie Murray's playing great at first, and Cal Ripken, Jr., is having an incredible rookie year!

P.P.P.S. "Underachiever guy" was an insult, wasn't it? Damn!

Dear Scott,

Well, if you were trying to ruin my day, it worked. And it has nothing to do with you being so obnoxious because you know more about music than me, although that didn't help. I mean, seriously, Scott—what's with the pregnancy jokes? Maybe you were trying to be funny, but you made me cry.

This is my third attempt to write back to you. I've been trying to remember what I could have written to upset you or to suggest that you are a loser like Todd Wilkerson. Unfortunately, I didn't make a photocopy of my letter, but I don't recall connecting you and Todd in any way whatsoever. The bottom line is that Todd is a loser who didn't go to college and works at a gas station. Not "because" he didn't go to college or "because" he works at a gas station. You and Todd are nothing alike. Nothing. You are smart and funny and interesting and . . . whatever. I'm too upset to pay you any more compliments. Todd is just so . . . Todd. Remember how he used to hang around the high school parking lot, just waiting for me to get out of school, and then all he'd want to do was sit in his basement and drink beer and watch TV? And he'd come to the football games and just go crazy, yelling and screaming at the other team, and then he got in that fight at the homecoming game? I mean, that's the stuff that made him a loser. You don't do that kind of stuff. At least I hope you don't.

You just write crappy letters to the girl who's supposed to be one of your closest friends! Seriously, Scott, you had to know that letter would hurt my feelings. And the pregnancy jokes? I'll give you five seconds to think about why I wouldn't find those funny. One, two, three, four, five. Got it. Oh, yeah, now you remember. Not so funny, is it? So cut the bullshit, okay?

I'm not in the mood to write anything cute or witty to you today. I'm too tired, I have a headache from crying, and I have that red, blotchy face thing going on, thanks to you. I just hope the puffiness goes away before the Pit closes so I can get dinner without everyone thinking I'm a homesick baby or something.

I'm still glad that you want to come see the English Beat with us. We got an extra ticket just to be on the safe side, and I'm sure your dad will let you out early to visit, particularly if you tell him that I'm upset with you right now. And guess what—you won't be lying!

And if he asks you how upset I am, tell him I'm so upset that I'm not even signing this letter, "Love, Catherine."

With vaguely positive emotions toward you at this moment, but secretly hoping you get the stomach flu,
Catherine

P.S. If you want to make sure that one of the two people in my dorm room talks to you when you visit, I'd advise you bring something from the East Bloomfield Quality Bakery, "Where Butter Makes the

Difference." (What a stupid motto.) Dorothy loves brownies. She's the brownie version of the Cookie Monster.

P.P.S. "Underachiever guy" isn't an insult. But I guess it's not exactly a compliment, either. It's a combination of the two. It's an "insultiment."

P.P.P.S. In the highly unlikely event that a lightning bolt strikes me dead as I am placing this letter in the mailbox, I'd hate for the last thing you'd remember to be a letter where I suggested that I don't care about you or wished you got the stomach flu. I do. You're just very difficult sometimes.

P.P.P.P.S. Go Orioles!

September 21, 1982

Dear Cath,

Or, "Dear, sweet, lovely, adorable, brilliant, looks-kind-of-cute-in-gym-shorts-but-not-as-cute-in-gym-shorts-as-Nancy-Gilmartin Cath." (Feel free to insert any adjectives I forgot.)

I'm so, so sorry about my last letter and about making you upset. Now I'm the one trying to figure out what I wrote because I also don't make photocopies of the letters I send you. I was feeling sorry for myself and obviously didn't explain what I was feeling in the right way. I didn't mean to blame you or suggest that you had called me a loser or thought that I was anything like Todd. I'm just not very good at writing my thoughts down, and I have the grades in English to prove it. (Actually, now that I think of it, since you did most of my English homework, *you* have the grades to prove it.)

If it makes you feel any better, now I feel terrible. I really look forward to your college girl letters. When I got the last one, I was excited until I opened it, then I felt terrible the entire night and couldn't sleep. I even tried to call you on the pay phone in your dorm, but some girl kept answering and hanging up right away.

So, if it's not already clear, I'm sorry. You're the last person on earth I'd want to hurt. Giving each other a hard time has always been our "thing"—sorry for the quotation marks—but maybe it's different when you do it in a letter. I'll try to be more careful about what I say and how I say it in the future.

And the pregnancy jokes? I wasn't thinking. I'm sorry about that, too.

Anyway, I hope you'll forgive me. I'll understand if you'd rather I not come down for that concert, and I'll understand if you think it's better if we stop writing to each other for a bit. You've got a lot to do at school, and I really should be working harder to take some pressure off my dad. If I don't hear from you for a while, that's cool—I'll see you when you come home in a few months for Thanksgiving, okay?

> With much more than vaguely positive feelings toward
> you at this moment,
> *Scott*

P.S. If I do come down, I will bring brownies. Although I may lick them all first.

P.P.S. Quick Orioles update: they're amazing. They're in second place now. I think they can catch the Brewers!

P.P.P.S. I'm enclosing a tape I made for you as a piece offering. It's got a bunch of English Beat songs on one side so you'll recognize them at the concert, and it's got that new Simple Minds album on the other side. The last song is a Kate Bush song called "Wuthering Heights" that I like. It reminds me of that book we were supposed to read junior year, and her voice reminds me of yours when you used to sing in the choir. I think you'll like it.

P.P.P.P.S. Hold on a second. Were we supposed to read *Wuthering Heights* or *Pride and Prejudice*? They're basically the same, right?

Dear Scott,

Thanks for your letter. We're fine. Sorry if I was overly sensitive about the pregnancy jokes. And maybe I was overly sensitive about some other stuff, too. It was mean of me to say that you're difficult. You're no more difficult than I am. And you've saved my proverbial ass too many times to count. (I'm afraid I don't know what proverb that's from, either.) And now you've introduced me to Kate Bush! She's amazing. I only wish I could sing like her.

Anyway, I expect to see you here for that English Beat concert. And, no, we don't need to stop writing to each other. I look forward to your letters, too, and Dorothy keeps begging me to let her read them. (Don't worry, that's not going to happen.) So let's just put this behind us and put it in the folder marked "Things We Don't Talk About," right next to that night at Burger King and the time you tried to grow a mustache.

I think you made an excellent point in your letter about how it may be different giving each other a hard time in writing than doing it in person. When we do it in writing, it's permanent and you can go back and read it over and over again and try to figure out the meaning. When we do it in person, you can see the other person and tell that they're joking or tell if their feelings are hurt.

That said, something good came out of our little miscommunication—College Boyfriend Number 1! His name is Walter. He's a junior. He saw that I was upset and came over to talk to me, and now we're dating! I'll tell you more about him soon. We're headed off to the Pit in a minute to get dinner together, so I need to wrap this up.

Love,
Cath

P.S. It's "peace" offering, not "piece" offering.

P.P.S. Oh, the girl who kept hanging up the phone every time you called? That was me. Sorry.

September 27, 1982

Dear Cath,

What?

    Scott

P.S. I knew it was you!

Dear Scott,

What do you mean, "What?" I know you haven't always liked them, but I've had a boyfriend pretty much constantly since eighth grade, so why are you so surprised? Plus, as I may have mentioned, it's your fault that Walter talked to me in the first place. I was sitting in Mag Court, near the bookstore and the campus post office, just staring into space, and he walked into my line of vision and said, "I've never seen you look sad before."

Good line, right? I'm embarassed to tell you about it, but I'm also smiling like an idiot just thinking about it. Anyway, he sat down, and I started talking to him about you and our friendship and how your letter had made me sad. So, yeah, we've been hanging out a lot since then and I think I really like him. I'm a little worried that I'm too impressed by him. He's introduced me to a bunch of his friends and fraternity brothers. Unlike most of my awkward freshman friends, Walter and his friends are very comfortable here, and everything they do seems cool. They have cars and live in upperclassman housing and know everything about everything. Of course, they also know about the English Beat and have tickets to the concert, so you'll get to meet Walter and some of his frat brothers. He said you can stay on their hall while you're visiting. I didn't really answer him when he offered. I mean, we've slept in each other's house so often, I don't think it will be a big deal for you to sleep on my dorm room floor, but I'll leave it up to you. Whatever makes you comfortable (and keeps you safe from Dorothy).

Speaking of Dorothy, I let her read your last letter. She was somewhat disappointed. You two are really going to hate each other. If it gets too bad, it might make sense for you to sleep at Walter's fraternity house.

Warning—here comes the boring part about school—Biology is kicking my ass. I'm already thinking about changing majors. To what, I don't know. That's it for the boring stuff.

I talked to my parents on Sunday. My dad gave me the "little princess" stuff again, but there must have been some mix-up because he said he didn't buy new pants at your dad's store. Is there another guy in town who looks exactly like my dad? Yikes! My mom said she sees you "all dressed up" and heading out to work all the time, so I assume that you see her, too. Would you please stop and talk to her once or twice before you come to visit so you can let me know how she is? I miss her so much and I feel guilty about leaving her home alone with my boring dad, regardless of whether he has new pants.

Oh, gross, Dorothy just came in with a big stinky pizza. Seriously, what do you put in a pizza to make it smell like that—sweat socks and Ben-Gay? I'm going to go hang out with Jane next door. Jane's cool, and her room doesn't reek of food all the time. Write soon, okay?

Much love,
Cath

P.S. Are you still a Tomato?

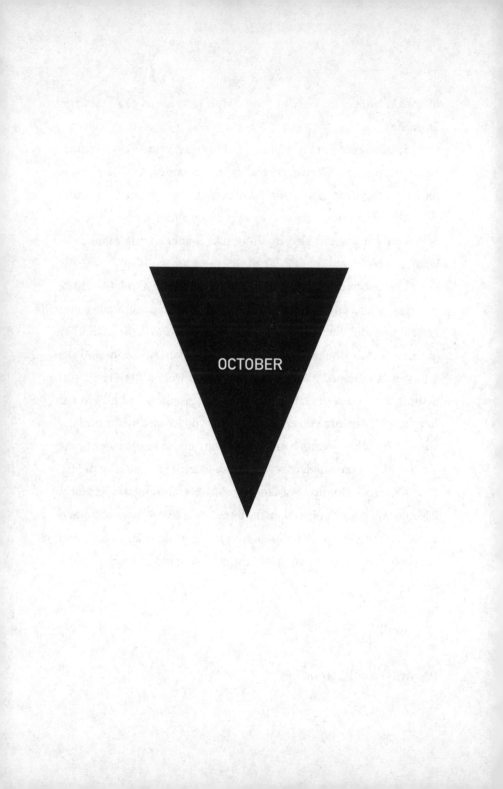

OCTOBER

October 1, 1982

Dear Cath,

I didn't mean "WHAT?" like I had no idea you'd ever had a boy-friend or thought the idea was inconceivable, but more like, "WHAT, where the hell did that come from?" because you hadn't mentioned any guys in your other letters, then, all of a sudden—boom, boyfriend!

Did that sentence even make sense? Could you tell that I had to stop to check how to spell "inconceivable"? Man, this letter-writing stuff is definitely not up my alley. It's much easier to talk to someone when they're in the same room with you. Know what I mean? And in our case, that will be very soon, thanks to the English Beat. (By the way, not to sound like an obnoxious know-it-all, but did you know that they're just called the Beat in England? They have to call themselves the English Beat here because there was already a band from Boston called the Beat. Was that obnoxious?)

I have to admit that the "I've never seen you look sad be-fore" line is a beauty. The only thing stopping me from using it is that you have to wait for a girl to look sad before you can try it out. That, or you have to hang out at places where sad girls hang out, and I have no idea where that would be. Maybe a library? Do we have a library in town? Is it that old building across from the post office where they hide all the books?

Sorry to hear about Biology. I have no advice for you about

41

that, but just felt it was important to reference it as proof that I read the whole letter and didn't skip the boring stuff.

Work is work. It's weird, but when I was in high school, I don't think I ever spoke with my dad for more than 10 minutes at a time, and even then it was only about the Orioles or the Colts. Now we work together all day. At first, we'd run out of things to talk about and I'd just go off somewhere and fold sweaters so it wouldn't be too awkward. But now, when the store's empty, we spend a lot of time just talking about things. It's funny how little I really knew about him. I mean, I knew he was in the Navy during the Korean War, but I didn't know he spent 18 months in a submarine. And I never knew anything about the sports he played in high school (track and lacrosse) or the women he dated before he met my mom. One was named Zelda, although I got the impression he might have been pulling my leg about her. Anyway, promise you won't tell him that I said this, but he's not that bad a guy. I can't believe you stole his car in high school to take your friends bar-hopping in Baltimore. Or was that me who did that?

By the way, that definitely was your dad who bought pants at the store. I even asked my dad, and he said of course it was. Maybe your dad misunderstood when you mentioned it, or maybe he just forgot. And I did see your mom after I got your letter. She was out in the garden, so I went to say hi. She seemed fine. Really. She said she missed you and that you don't write enough. Then she used the "F-word." (Kidding, I'm kidding.)

I'll try to call you in the next couple days so we can firm up the plans for my visit to Virginia, or South Carolina, or Guam, or wherever you go to school.

Talk to you soon.

Scott

P.S. Do you remember when Joe and I sang that Pretenders song at the Senior Talent Show? Give me your honest answer—do you think I should think about starting a band? I mean, I'm not bad on the guitar, and everyone liked the song we sang. I'm not saying I'm great, but it could be fun, and maybe we could play at some bars or something. And if there are some sad girls there, I could try out that line on them!

P.P.S. The Orioles are only two games behind the Brewers with three games to go! And all three games are against the Brewers at Memorial Stadium! If they can win all three, they'll win the pennant! So it could all come down to the game Sunday afternoon. And my dad got us tickets to the game on Sunday afternoon! He's actually going to close the store early so we can be there! Pretty cool, huh?

P.P.P.S. Are you still a Potato?

Dearest Scottie-Scott-Scott,

What a sweet, normal letter! Thank you. And yes, I'm still a Potato! And I will be until the day I fry. And I'm looking forward to seeing you. I've been a bundle of nerves, and it will be such a relief to have a friend from home to hang out with.

I can't believe you brought up the library as a place to meet girls (and yes, that old building across from the post office is indeed a library, which you would know if I hadn't done ALL the research for that affirmative action debate we had last year). I had been hearing rumors and stories about the main library here on campus, "the Z" (short for "the Z. Smith Reynolds Library"), like about how certain sororities and fraternities only study in a certain reading room and how you're supposed to go to the huge rooms full of rows of books, "the stacks," if you really need to concentrate and study, and then I also heard that people fool around in the stacks, which strikes me as gross, but whatever. I'd been too intimidated to even go to the Z because I'd been afraid of sitting in the wrong place or rounding a corner to find some couple boinking someplace where I wasn't supposed to be.

But then yesterday, after I'd been saying how I had to study for a Biology test, Walter asked me if I want to study in the stacks with him! I didn't know WHAT he meant, you know? But I didn't want to be a complete dork, so I said sure, that sounds great. What a mistake that was! He saunters through the various reading rooms and up one of the many internal metal staircases to some damp, dimly lit, remote corner of what feels like an airplane hangar full of dusty books, which make me sneeze repeatedly, and I proceed to read the same paragraph over and over again without comprehending a single word because I'm such a nervous wreck. Walter meanwhile is holding court and receiving what feels like a never-ending stream of sorority girl visitors. They were amazingly polite and rude at the same time. The introductions were all the same. Blazing smile, head tilt to drape the hair over one shoulder, "Hi!", odd blink, followed by a subtle turn to dismiss me and pour all their hormones directly onto Walter. After two or three of them, I figured out that the odd blink wasn't actually a blink, but an amazingly quick up-down to check out just who Walter was with. It was completely disconcerting, and I had to claim to be tired so I could go home and stay up for several more hours to try to actually, you know, *study.* I still couldn't really concentrate, though, because I was thinking, "Well, at least he didn't try to make out with me in that gross place." And then I thought, "But is that because I didn't fit in with those girls, or because he obviously likes one of them better, or did he go off and fool around with one of them when he said he went to the bathroom?" which, yes, I know is ridiculous, but you get my point!

BORING PARAGRAPH ALERT! Needless to say, the Biology test did not go well. On the upside, I'm doing pretty well in everything else.

Getting back to your letter, yes, I definitely think you should start a band! You and Joe were great doing "Kid" at the Senior Talent

Show. (You didn't think I'd remember the name of the song, did you?) And I think you'd have fun. Whenever there's a band at a party here, the girls basically just argue about who's the sexiest guy in the band. And the singers sometimes change the lyrics to flirt with the girls in front of everyone, which they LOVE, so yeah, I think that's a great idea, and I'm sure you'll meet lots of girls that way. Plus, you'll know right away that you have at least one thing in common, which is that you'd both think that you're pretty sexy. Ha ha!

Thank you for telling me about seeing my mom in the garden. Can I assume she was planting her fall pansies? She always says that seeing their faces looking up at her makes her happy, and it makes me happy to think of her enjoying those simple things again. I'll try to write her more often. It's a little difficult because I can't be totally honest with her about everything that goes on here, but please tell her that I'm thinking of her and that I miss her a lot. And please don't tell her that Walter took me down to the stacks, even though nothing happened!

I'm glad things are getting easier between you and your dad. You can tell me more about it on your visit. I'm enclosing a map of the campus with my dorm circled so you can find it. Please note that it's in NORTH CAROLINA. The campus is really beautiful and I know you are going to love it here! I can't wait to see you. We'll have to take lots of walks to get away from Dorothy, and I want us to hang out with Jane. She's really my best girlfriend here.

Before I forget, you're going to have to tell everyone here about Donnie Dibsie's "We Will Always Be Tornadoes" graduation speech because half the people here don't get it and the other half think I'm making it up! Who could make THAT up? Mark Twain couldn't have made that up! (Mark Twain wrote a bunch of books you were supposed to read in high school.)

Say "hi" to your mom and dad (no head tilt required).

Much love from the girl who did not steal your dad's car,
Cath

P.S. Sorry to hear about the Orioles. I read in the paper about the last game of the season. 10–2, huh? And Jim Palmer gave up a bunch of homers. Hope you and your dad aren't too disappointed, but it must have been really exciting to see them get so close again.

P.P.S. Jim Palmer's the cute one in the Hanes underwear ads, right?

October 7, 1982

Dear Cath,

Depending on how fast the mail is, you may or may not get this letter before I see you on Saturday. Did you say your school is in North Carolina or South Carolina? I'll flip a coin.

I'm looking forward to visiting. I've even been practicing Donnie Dipshit's dipshitty graduation speech. "No matter where we go, no matter what we do, whether we are successes or failures, whether we change the world or only change our little piece of it, there is one thing no one will ever be able to take away from us, one thing that will bind us together for eternity—we are the East Bloomfield High School Tornadoes, Class of 1982. And we will always be Tornadoes!" Pretty good, huh?

My parents are giving me fifty bucks to take you out to dinner. They may or may not want you to sign a sworn statement confirming that I in fact took you out to dinner with the money. If I show up Saturday with a notary public, I hope you'll understand why.

I don't know what to say about that experience you had in the library with Walter and the sorority girls. It seems strange to me, but I have no idea how sorority girls act. I only know what sorority girls are because I saw *Animal House* half a dozen times. (They're pretty, blond, big-chested girls who wear tight sweaters, right? I'm joking, but if I'm right, I hope you'll have some time to give me a tour of some of the sorority houses during my visit. Or maybe just drop me off.) Anyway, I'm not very good at giving advice, and you haven't asked for my advice, but, if you did, I'd suggest you just ask Walter what the heck that library thing was all about. (Were there too many commas in that sentence? It feels like there were too many, doesn't it?)

I talked with Joe, and he's definitely interested in starting a band with me. We've decided that I'm going to play lead guitar and be the lead singer, and he's going to play rhythm guitar and sing the backup vocals. There's a guy he works with at the supermarket who plays the bass, so we're going to give him a tryout. As for the drums, the only person we can think of who plays the drums is . . . your old boyfriend Todd Wilkerson. We haven't asked him if he's interested in joining our band yet because I told Joe I wanted to run it by you first. If you have a problem with it, just let me know. But he's a pretty good drummer, and he has a van.

We've already come up with a few ideas for the name of our band. What do you think of these:

1) Kiss This
2) The Daydreamers
3) Thrill Ride
4) Accelerator
5) Scott and the Tornadoes
6) Joe and the Tornadoes
7) I've Seen Cath's Underwear (just seeing if you're paying attention, but it's true)

8) The Mirrors

9) The Incredible Mirrors

10) Shrinking Star

11) The Blue Engines

12) Ouch

Number 6 is the worst of the bunch. Who ever heard of a band being named after the rhythm guitarist? (Answer: No one.) Not to poison the well, but you should know that I like numbers 9 and 11 the best.

I don't want to talk about the Orioles or about Jim Palmer's underwear.

See you in Florida in a couple days.

Scott

P.S. Are you still a Torpedo?

October 11, 1982

Dear Scott,

Did you really need to get in a fight with my boyfriend AND make out with my roommate?

One or the other just wasn't enough for you? You had to do BOTH?

Jesus. I mean, JESUS!

Cath

October 14, 1982

Cath—

Excuse me, but *I* started a fight with your boyfriend? *I* started it? *Me?* You have to be fucking kidding me. I spent an entire weekend taking abuse from your rich, pretentious snob of a boyfriend Walter ("It's not Walt, it's Walter") while you just sat there smiling, and somehow I'm to blame because I finally stuck up for myself? And don't say he wasn't giving me a hard time, okay? How many sentences did he start with "If you were familiar with philosophy," or "If you were familiar with economics," or "If you were familiar with some of the basic concepts of whatever"? Oh, I've got a better one—"Yes, I'm sure that comes up often in a clothing store." Nice. Very nice.

Listen, I know you like this guy, but how difficult would it have been for you to have said, "Walter, not Walt, this is one of my closest friends since I was 5 years old. I've known him for 13 years. I've known you for 3 minutes. So you need to chill out." Would that have killed you?

As for making out with your roommate, why the hell do you care? I don't tell you who you shouldn't make out with. But if I did, the first name on the list would begin with a *W.* If you were familiar with the basic concepts of whatever, you'd know I was referring to Walter, not Walt.

So if you're looking for an apology, you're barking up the

wrong tree this time, college girl. I drove for seven hours just to see you. I didn't expect to be treated like crap.

   Scott

P.S. And even if I did start a fight with your boyfriend—which I didn't—how many fights did you start with Samantha? A hundred? A *thousand*?

P.P.S. I'm asking Todd to be our drummer. I didn't have to ask your permission. You're not my mother. I don't know what you are right now.

Dear Scott,

I'm really sorry that the visit went so badly. When you pull those sentences out of the conversation, I can see why you got so upset. I kind of thought that Walter was just trying to include you in the conversation. Like when everybody was talking about the stress of getting ready for mid-terms and he said something about the stress of working in a store during the holidays, I thought he was trying to be nice and trying to bring you into the conversation. He's usually pretty smooth socially. Maybe I'm too starry-eyed about him, but I don't think he meant to be a jerk. I'm sorry, I really wanted to show you the good things about college and to just have a nice time hanging out together.

Looking back on it, though, I can see how awkward it was for you, and I'm sorry we didn't just spend more time by ourselves or in a smaller group. I wish you hadn't stormed back to the dorm by yourself. In hindsight I see that I should have gone with you, if for no other reason than to keep you from running into Dorothy. Which, by the way, we really need to talk about. Not like really *talk* about, because I have no interest in ever reliving any aspect of opening my dormroom door to find you in Dorothy's bed. God knows I would scrub my eyeballs and my brainpan with bleach if I thought it would erase the image, so let's please please please never discuss that again. However, you do need to do something about the overall situation, because you have created a crazy (crazier?) person who happens to live five feet away from me. To update you on the crazy meter: she has taken down the HANG IN THERE, BABY poster and replaced it with an English Beat poster; she springs like a cat and sprints out of the room whenever the hall phone rings and then tries to be super cool when she answers it ("Hu-llooo?"); she painted her nails black and has gone totally overboard on the eyeliner; and she stopped bringing her stinky pizzas back to our dorm room every day. For the last one, I thank you, but for the rest, I say you'd better do something to manage the situation, my friend. You seem to have left her with the distinct impression that she's your *girl*friend and that you are some sort of hard-assed rocker dude. Judging from the tone of your last letter and the fact that you've got Todd on drums, maybe you have become a hard-assed rocker dude, but let's all admit that Dorothy is not really your girlfriend, shall we? And perhaps clear that up sooner rather than later, okay, because she is hinting around about coming home with me for Thanksgiving, and if you don't start being nice to me again, I may just let her tag along.

Well, I don't know where to go from here, so I'll just sign off with:

1. I really am sorry we didn't have a better visit; and
2. I hope we can still hang out at Thanksgiving (without Dorothy). My mother would be confused and devastated if you didn't join us for leftovers on Friday.

Still your friend(?),
Cath

October 21, 1982

Cath,

What?

Or, to put it more accurately, WHAT?!?!

Or, as they would say in France, WHAT THE FUCK?!?!?! (Sorry, but I didn't pay much attention in French.)

I just had to go back and reread your letter to make sure I didn't misread it or to see if maybe you were joking.

You're not joking, are you?

Dorothy thinks she's my girlfriend?

Your roommate Dorothy, who I fooled around with once when I was drunk, thinks she's my girlfriend?

Your roommate Dorothy, whose last name I don't even know, thinks she's my girlfriend?

Dorothy, who would know my last name only if you happened to tell her, thinks she's my girlfriend?

Dorothy, who wouldn't even know how to contact me unless you gave her my address and phone number, thinks she's my girlfriend?

WHAT THE FUCK?!?!?

Sorry to break out the French again, but that is absolutely, completely, 100% batshit insane.

Look, I know that weekend was horrible for too many reasons to mention, but I give you my word of honor as a Tornado that I didn't do anything to even suggest to Dorothy that our, ahem, encounter was anything more than one very drunk guy fooling around with one lonely sober girl with a HANG IN THERE, BABY poster over her bed. We just happened to be in the same place at the same time. Yes, we fooled around, but we didn't . . . I don't even want to say it, so kindly make a ring with the thumb and index finger of your left hand and poke the index finger of your right hand in and out of it a few times. You know what I mean. Think of the last week of our Sex Ed class. We didn't do *that*.

I was about to write that this will be easy for me to handle because I live hundreds of miles away and she doesn't know how to reach me, except for the fact that SHE JUST CALLED WHILE I WAS WRITING THIS STUPID LETTER TO YOU. At least I assume it's her because my mom just popped in to say that Dorothy Golper is on the phone for me. Is that her? Golper? I made out with a Golper? Anyway, I told my mom to tell her that I'm out for the night.

Give me a call when you get this so we can discuss how I should handle this. If she weren't your roommate, I'd probably just dodge her calls or tell her she's mistaken about the whole girlfriend thing, but I apreciate that might make things messy for you. And while making things messy for you is normally something I'd be very interested in, and which has some appeal after having to deal with that Walter jerk, I'll try not to do it this one time. If you want to call me during the day, you can call me at the store. It's dead until 3 p.m. most week-days.

> Take care,
> *Scott*

P.S. I wrote two new songs for the band last night. Just the lyrics, but I have the music in my head. Let me know if you want me to share the lyrics.

P.P.S. Please note that I didn't say a single bad thing about your boyfriend in this entire letter. Oh, hold on, I just reread the letter and I did.

P.P.P.S. Golper? Seriously?

October 25, 1982

Dear Scott,

Oh my gosh, it was so good to talk to you last night! How typical of us that you drive all the way down here, everything is weird, and then we have a great conversation on the phone. Next time let's just skip the weirdness, okay?

Maybe you were just trying to be upbeat because I was getting emotional about my family stuff, but it sounds like things are going much better for you at the store. I knew your dad's positive attitude would rub off on you and you would start to enjoy it more. And yes, you should definitely play at the Morrisons' party over Thanksgiving weekend if you think your band will be ready by then. It's not a lot of time, but I think all of our high school friends are really looking forward to being home and getting together at that party. I'm sure they would love to see your band. The song lyrics that you read to me on the phone were great, and it would be really cool to mix in some of your original stuff with the classics from high school.

Are you doing anything fun for Halloween? Buckle your seat belt, because I have some pretty fun plans to tell you about—I'll be WORKING on Halloween. Yep. No joke. I forgot to tell you last night, but I got a job twirling pizza dough. And then spreading sauce on it. And then usually covering it with pepperoni and cheese. Jane and I decided we need some spending money, so we got jobs at the Pizza Pan in the basement of the dorm across the quad. Sometimes we make pizza and sometimes we deliver it. Or, I should say, sometimes

I deliver it. On her first delivery, Jane had to go to a boys' dorm and was all nervous and jittery about being surrounded by cute boys. She spun around too quickly with a pizza box in her hand and the pizza flew out of the box like a Frisbee. She was horrified and ran out of there crying while the pizza slid down the wall, and now I take her turns as well as my own on the delivery rotation. Here are some fun facts about delivering pizza on a college campus: Boys who want pizza past 9 p.m. invariably live on the third floor of a building that doesn't have an elevator or air-conditioning, are stoned out of their minds, don't have any money for tips, and are stupid enough to offer me a bong hit or a beer as a tip instead. Girls on the other hand just grab the box, yell "Thanks!" and slam the door. No tips there, either, but at least we avoid the awkward bong hit conversation. I don't know who I love more.

So all roads seem to lead us back to pizza-eating girls. (And yes, The Golper's pizza-eating has resumed. With a vengeance.) To follow up on what we talked about last night, you really, really do need to write a "Dear Dorothy" letter. Just make something up. A girlfriend. A boyfriend. Whatever. Just get her to stop going through my stuff for tidbits of information about you and weeping through her black eyeliner. I know that's mean, but I'm worried that she's going to pick up the phone when my mom calls and somehow cajole her way into a Thanksgiving weekend invitation. She's very good at seeming cheerful and pathetic all at the same time. ("Oh, Mrs. Osteen, that care package you sent to Catherine was so lovely!

I wish *my* mother was as thoughtful as you are! Oh, no, I can't afford to go home for the holidays, but they say the turkey in the Pit isn't *that* bad.") Can you imagine me rolling into the Morrisons' house with her in tow? That would certainly put an interesting spin on the evening.

I get my paycheck this Friday and may try to come home the weekend after next. Thanksgiving is so late this year, I don't really want to wait that long. Could you maybe pick me up at the bus station in Baltimore?

Off to the Z for some calculus homework (wanted to throw that in so you could go right to sleep after reading this letter).

Much love,
Cath

P.S. Should I be worried that Walter (not Walt) is super excited about his fraternity's annual Halloween party even though I can't go because I'll be working?

P.P.S. You have no interest in giving me any advice about Walter, do you?

P.P.P.S. Are we back on good enough terms that I can tell you that the word "appreciate" has two *P*s in it and we'll still be friends?

October 28, 1982

Cath—

Great to talk to you the other night, too. And that's cool that you got a job at that pizza place. You'll have to sneak a pizza or two out next time I visit. Sausage and peppers on top, please.

Of course I'd be happy to pick you up at the bus station in Baltimore when you come home—but only if you are alone. If you're bringing Walter home for the weekend, well, it might make sense for me to keep my distance. Same thing if you're bringing Dorothy. (However, if you are bringing that cute blond girl named Wendy, then I would be pleased to come pick you both up at the bus station. In fact, if you feel like you need to spend time with your parents, you are more than welcome to have her stay at our place for the weekend. More than welcome. Much, much more than welcome. Extremely welcome. Have I made my point? May I stop now?)

Speaking of Dorothy, I have written three "Dear Dorothy" letters, which I will enclose. Please let me know which one you think would work the best. Until then, I will not be answering the phone.

Regarding your question about Walter and his fraternity's Halloween party, I'm sure your boy Walter is just excited about the party because he and his buddies will be rubbing olive oil all over each other and then wrestling on the kitchen floor. That's what those frat guys do, right?

And speaking of wrestling on the floor, what's the story with that girl Wendy? Where's she from? Is she dating anyone? Has she ever dated a rock star/clothing salesman?

By the way, our band's new name is Crush. It has a double meaning. It can mean "crush" like destroying something, but it can also mean "crush" like having a crush on someone. I'm working on designing a logo for the band, too. Eventually, we'll get around to playing some music. It's important to put the cart before the horse, don't you think? First the name and the logo, then the music. I'll bet that's how the Beatles did it.

Oh, speaking of music, have you heard the new album by Prince? It's called *1999*. I've never heard anything like it. The title song is really funky, and you'll absolutely love a song called "Little Red Corvette." Hint: it's not really about a little red Corvette. Let me know if you want me to make a tape of it for you.

Talk to you soon.

Scott

Dear Dorothy,

I have just returned from the doctor, and he tells me that I have something called "herpes." It's pronounced "her-peas." I'm afraid I wasn't really paying attention while he was talking, so I don't know what it is, but it sounds cool, don't you think?

I can't wait to come down to see you again so we can take our relationship to another level!

Very truly yours,
Scott

Dearest Dorothy,

It is with mixed feelings that I must tell you that I have decided to enlist in the United States Marine Corps. I am shipping out as soon as I put this letter in the mail.

I will think of you often, but believe it is important for you to forget about me and move on. Yes, move on and don't ever look back. That's what I want for you.

If you should happen to call my house and hear a voice that sounds like mine, that's my dad.

And if someone should visit Cath who looks like me and answers to the same name, that's also my dad. He's very young looking and apparently very close to Cath. And apparently his name is Scott, too.

I wish you the best of luck. Now I'm off to Vietnam.

Sincerely,
Scott

P.S. Also, I have herpes.

Dear Dorothy,

It would be easier for me to say this if I had herpes or was joining the Marines, but I feel that I must end our relationship.

Because I have syphilis.

And I'm joining the Army.

Good luck to you.

Good-bye.

Scott

NOVEMBER

November 1, 1982

Dear Scott,

I have officially learned three new things about my life at college.

1. Do not open and read your letters anywhere near my dormitory. I thought I was being safe by reading your latest letter (or letters, some might say) in the courtyard outside my dorm. However, due to your ridiculous sense of humor, I was laughing so hard that The Golper must have seen me from our window, and she came busting out the front door yelling "What's so funny?! Did you get a letter from Scott?!! YOU HAVE TO SHOW IT TO ME!!!" At which point, I scrambled around like a spider picking up my stuff and saying something along the lines of "What? Whoa, hey, yeah, NO!" and ran away. Literally, I ran away from my roommate and am hiding in the stacks of the library, where, I am happy to report, no one is having sex at this moment.

2. Keep up with the reading lists. I will likely be spending a lot of time here in the stacks since (a) you have driven my roommate insane, and (b) college midterms cover a lot of material. I don't know what I was thinking when I said I might come home next weekend. Especially now that I have a job, I am way behind on everything, and I'll need to stay here until Thanksgiving. Super boring, I know. Plus, my mom was acting weird about me coming home. Not like she didn't want to see me, exactly, she just wasn't really enthusiastic about it.

3. If you have a cute, popular, fraternity boyfriend, don't leave

him alone at a Halloween party with drunk girls dressed as French maids, or you may have to break up with him the next day.

So, yeah, bottom line, I'll be spending a lot of time hiding out here in the stacks, not having sex. Super depressing, I know.

I like the name Crush. You're right, it has lots of meanings.

Miss you,
College Girl

P.S. Jane picked up the new Prince album the day it came out. I agree with you, it's fantastic. And I think you're right that "Little Red Corvette" isn't really about a little red Corvette. I don't think "little red Corvette" even qualifies as a double entendre. I think it's a single entendre.

November 3, 1982

Cath—

Sorry my last letter almost got you in trouble with your roommate. But you'll be happy to know that she hasn't called me at all this past week. Although someone keeps calling and hanging up whenever one of my parents answers the phone. Hmm, I wonder who that could be.

Anyway, much more importantly, did you break up with Walter? Did he cheat on you at that Halloween party? Would you like me to kick the snot out of him? I will gladly come visit for the sole purpose of kicking the snot out of that weasel. Just say the word. Any word.

I believe this is where I'm supposed to tell you that you can do better than that guy. Well, you can do better than that guy. I mean, come on. He's a shitheel. You're a Tornado.

Things here are fine. We've been rehearsing a couple hours a night after work, and we're starting to sound pretty good, if I do say so myself. Joe and Todd went with me to Music Land on Sunday afternoon, and I bought a used Fender Stratocaster. It's the same model Eric Clapton uses. The one I bought has a small crack in it that they had to repair, so I got it for a good price.

So far, we've mostly been playing covers of songs we like, but I'm taking a crack at writing a few songs myself. The one I really like so far is called "Sometimes, Samantha Drew." (Yes, I used Samantha's name. I'll probably change it. Probably.) It's about a guy who misses his girlfriend after she moves out. It goes like this:

I get up in the morning,
And go to work in the mill,
I come home in the evening,
And wonder if you will.
I wake up in the evening,
In the wee wee hours,
Wondering if you'll come back to
This house of ours.
Sometimes, Samantha Drew,
Do you think of me?
Sometimes, Samantha Drew.
I still think of you.

Before you say it, I already know what you're going to say: "Um, Scott, what do you know about working in a mill?" The answer is, "Nothing." But if you think anyone wants to hear a song that begins, "I wake up in the morning and go to work at the boys and men's clothing store my father owns," I think you're very, very wrong.

And you're also going to say something about me using the words "wee wee hours," aren't you? It's supposed to remind you of a Frank Sinatra song called "In the Wee Small Hours of the Morning." If you aren't familiar with the song, I guess it will remind you of urination. Po-TAY-toe, po-TAH-toe, as my mom would say. Usually when she's serving potatoes.

Maybe I'll record one of our next rehearsals and send you a cassette. Of course, if you listen to it in your dorm room, you'll have to tell your roommate that it's my father's band. Because I'm still serving my country in a foreign land while tending to my disease-ridden genitals.

(I am hereby copyrighting the name "Disease Ridden Genitals" in case I ever decide to form a punk band. So don't go around using it, okay?)

I have to end this so I can head off to the mill. Talk to you soon.

Scott

P.S. Seriously, say the word.

Dear Scott,

I hope it goes without saying that "Disease Ridden Genitals" is the worst name of all time for a band. But, oddly, it would be a perfect name for a boy if you ever get married and have a son. Just saying.

I really like your lyrics, but I think you should change the name. I'm sorry, I know you miss Samantha a lot, even if you don't say it, and I know she and her boobs meant a lot to you, but she broke up with you, Scott. Having her name in the song makes you sound like you can't get over her. People will wonder if you're just sitting around at home fixating on Samantha. And, more importantly, she doesn't *deserve* to have a song written about her. She just doesn't. So, yeah, change the name, and send me the tape of the rehearsal because the music part can make or break a song like that.

I'll apologize for the rest of this letter, Scott, because I don't have much happy news. Yes, I did break up with Walter (which, ultimately, is the best news I have to tell you). Unfortunately for him, there are professional photographers at most of the fraternity and sorority dances. They are really efficient about developing and posting copies of the party pictures so the happy partygoers can order copies of themselves having fun, fun, fun. It was hard for Walter to pretend that he didn't have a blast without me when he's got a different girl on his lap, in his arms, or practically sitting on his face in every picture. It was so humiliating to walk around campus the next day and see girls glance at me and then quickly look away to

73

laugh and share those wide-eyed knowing looks among themselves. You were right about Walter-not-Walt all along. He and one of his "brothers" stumbled upon me in the library the other day and, for reasons I will explain in a minute, my eyes were bloodshot from crying. Walter tried to seem all concerned while his "brother" actually smirked and looked away. In that moment, I saw them so clearly as the shitheels that they really are—I'm stealing "shitheels" from you—and it was somewhat satisfying to just stare at them until they went away.

The real bad news, other than my Biology midterm grade, is that the rumors about my dad and his slutty secretary are true. After all the months of denying it, he has now admitted that he's the one who got her pregnant. Can you believe it? My mom waited until after midterms to tell me so I wouldn't tank my grades. She is so torn up about everything. I've never heard a grown person sob like that. It's why she was so weird about me trying to come home before—she didn't want me there while my dad was moving out. She said he's moved out in little bits and pieces so the neighbors wouldn't notice. He didn't want to make a "scene." How awesome is that? He made a baby, but he doesn't want to make a scene. I don't know if your parents know or not. I want my mom to talk to some friends about it, but she is really embarrassed and hurt. She's normally such a classy lady, and now she just doesn't know what to do.

Anyway, I'm kind of a wreck. Breaking up with Walter was

good timing because people just assume that I'm sad and weepy because of him when, actually, I am really upset about my dad and worried about my mom and freaking out in general about what it's going to be like to come home to a half-empty house at Thanksgiving. I've been trying to call my mom more often, and I think she's been drinking sometimes at night. She wants to just rant and rave about my dad, and it's awkward for me because I'm sitting in the hall of my dorm with people stepping over me or waiting to use the phone. She can't seem to keep my work schedule straight and gets mad if I don't call her on my work nights, even though I told her I couldn't call because of work. And of course The Golper is way too nosy about all the long-distance calls and clearly thinks that I have stolen you from her. I've given up trying to dissuade her. It's just not worth the energy, and I spend most of my free time in Jane's room anyway.

I have to run and deliver pizzas soon. On a positive note in this otherwise sickening letter, I can say that I really like my job now. It's nice to get paid to mindlessly walk around campus alone at night. And it tires me out climbing so many stairs and logging so many miles doing my deliveries. My mind is racing so much that I can't sleep these days unless I'm really exhausted, and delivering pizzas all over campus does get pretty exhausting.

Anyway, please help me at Thanksgiving, okay? It's hard to imagine what will be worse. Seeing my dad or not seeing my dad. And if I do see him, he better not be with his slutty, pregnant secretary or wearing some new pants that he bought at your dad's store and lied about for some unknown reason. I mean, why would you lie about buying a fucking pair of pants? Does the guy lie about everything?

Not at my best,
Cath

November 7, 1982

Dear Cath,

Holy shit.

Or, more accurately, HOLY SHIT!

I am speechless. I have lost the ability to speak.

Literally an hour has passed since I wrote that last sentence, and all I can think of to say is HOLY SHIT!

I just tried to call you, but your roommate answered. I had to pretend it was a wrong number.

Okay, it's been another half hour. HOLY SHIT!

Let me share my thoughts with you in no particular order.

Walter is a douche.

Your dad is a super-douche.

Sorry, but it's true.

When you first told me last summer about the rumors that your dad got his secretary pregnant, my reaction was that there was no way in hell and that people were just being gossipy because they have nothing better to do in this suckful town. I mean, the guy goes to church every Sunday and is always busting my chops about how I don't go. Plus, he dresses so conservatively, and, sorry, but he's fat and practically bald. Who would think any woman (except your mom) would find him attractive, let alone a girl in her twenties. So there was no way he got her pregnant, right? It seemed like just a stupid rumor.

But now? Now your dad is a super-douche. He should have

77

to wear a red *S* on his chest the rest of his life, like the lady in the movie *The Scarlet Letter*.

I would have told you if I'd noticed anything unusual going on at your house, but I've noticed nothing. NOTHING. If your parents have been fighting, I haven't seen it. And if your dad has been moving out, I haven't seen that either. No suitcases or boxes or anything. Things looked perfectly normal at your house except for the fact that you're not there and your mom's been walking your dog. But now I'm looking out the window and—guess what—your dad's car isn't in the driveway, where it normally would be at this time.

And the pants! It's driving me crazy. Why would he lie about buying a pair of pants at my dad's store? Oh my God, I just thought of it. I'll bet he was with his secretary, and he got something on his pants, and he had to replace them so your mom wouldn't ask any questions about the stain on his pants! And then he had to lie about it because otherwise he'd have to explain why he replaced his pants! That makes sense, doesn't it?

I just tried to call you again, and your roommate answered again! Does she wait by the phone all day? Does she ever go to classes? Jesus!

I don't know what else to say, Cath. Did I mention your dad's a super-douche? Yeah, I guess I did. But it's worth repeating. What a super-douche. Next time he gives me a hard time about not going to church, I'm going to tell him to go screw himself. Sorry, but I will.

Listen, I'm going to come visit you this Tuesday so we can talk about this. I've already told my dad I need to take the day off, and I had to explain what's happened. I hope you don't mind, but my dad wants to beat the crap out of your dad, if that makes you feel any better. And he gave me some money to take you to lunch. We might have to meet off campus or something so I don't have to deal with your roommate, but I'll be there Tuesday morning. You can count on me. I'll keep trying to call you so we can at least talk a bit and make plans where to meet.

In the meantime, take some advice from your roommate's old poster and HANG IN THERE, BABY.

Scott

P.S. HOLY MOTHERFUCKING SHIT!

P.P.S. You're probably right about changing the name in the song. But I suspect Samantha will probably come back home next summer, and who knows what will happen if we spend the summer together. Then if she moves back after she graduates, anything could happen.

November 10, 1982

Dear Scott,

You were incredibly sweet to drive all the way down here to spend the day with me yesterday. It was so nice to get off campus and walk around town with you. I didn't realize how much I needed to talk. And cry. And talk and cry. I'm sorry the waitress yelled at you for "breaking up with me" at Colson's when I was crying, although watching you try to figure out what the hell she was talking about was kind of worth it. Southern women get passionate about break-ups. Maybe it's all that country music they listen to. It seems like it's all about breaking up and making up. It's like you know the lyrics the first time you hear the song.

Sorry, I'm sort of rambling here. I should confess that I accepted some pizza delivery "tips" that were offered to me tonight and I've had a few beers. Maybe more than a few beers. Although I don't really know how many beers you would consider to be "a few." What a goofy phrase that is. WHATEVER, I'm buzzed and writing a letter to a friend on a Wednesday night. Woo hoo!

Anyway, thank you again for coming to see me. It was a big relief to be able to talk to you. You are probably the one person on the planet who understands what a total shock this is. It's not just like some cliché, like some suave dude hooking up with his secretary. *It's my dad.* My nerdy, kind-of-fat dad with a corny sense of humor and an ugly Christmas sweater. He's the guy who's always telling me about right and wrong. Sometimes actually yelling at me about right and wrong. Sometimes shaking his head in despair that "the world is going to hell in a handbasket!" And my poor mother. Jesus, Mary, and Joseph. We talked about her yesterday, but really, what the hell is she going to do? She hasn't worked in 20 years! And what am I supposed to do? Should I come home? Should I transfer to the University of Maryland so I'll be closer to home? Should I take a year off? Hey, maybe your dad would give me a job. I would need a job. My mom is FREAKING OUT about money. You and I would have fun working together, though. But we would also probably get fired if we worked together.

Okay, I have to go to bed now. I'm sorry for that greasy spot on the page. I think I fell asleep for a little while.

You're a good friend for a guy. I don't know what I would do without you.

Cath

P.S. I don't know how to break this to you, but Samantha isn't moving back to East Bumfuck, Maryland, after she graduates from college. Sorry, but she's been itching to get out of there for a while.

P.P.S. Also, I know you "visited" with Dorothy while I was delivering pizzas yesterday. I'm biting my tongue.

November 12, 1982

Cath,

It was great to see you, too.

You're probably right that Samantha's not moving back here after college. I mean, why would she? There's nothing to do here, and it's not like she went off to college so she could just come back here and work at the grocery store again.

As for me and Dorothy, just shut up, okay? I have no interest in talking about it other than to say that if you hadn't gone to work a shift at that pizza place, NOTHING WOULD HAVE HAPPENED. So any blame falls squarely on your pretty, oddly small head.

As for how many beers would qualify as "a few," I would say four. Which, if I remember correctly, was your record back in high school. Did you break your record? And was it better beer than the National Bohemian we used to get from Duffy's when Claire was working there?

As for the most important subject—your super-douche of a dad—I'm not sure there's anything more I can say that I didn't say on Tuesday. Your dad's a super-douche, your mom's a nice lady, it sucks that your dad would do that to her, it sucks that your dad would do that to YOU, and, in case I hadn't mentioned it, your dad is a super-douche. I'm sorry I can't think of anything new to say. And I'm sorry you're dealing with this. But I wouldn't do anything drastic if I were you. No need to drop out of school or come home, and certainly no need to work at a men's clothing store. You haven't sunk that low yet.

I was thinking about your situation on the incredibly long drive home—traffic was a nightmare on I-95—and I ended up writing a song about it in my head. I need to write it down on paper when I have a moment. It's actually a pretty good song, I think, but I'm not sure if you'd like it, so I'm going to keep it to myself for now.

I'll try to give you a call soon.

Say hello to Dorothy for me. (Shut up!)

Scott

P.S. By the way, my dad is incredibly worked up about this whole thing with your dad. Not sure why, but he is. He said your dad came into the store again on Tuesday afternoon, and it was all he could do not to punch your dad in the face. I don't mean to sound like a child here, but I'm pretty sure my dad could beat up your dad. I mean, my dad was in the military. Your dad was in the chess club. Case closed.

Dear Scott,

I'm sorry you got stuck in traffic on the way home. I really do appreciate you rushing down here and understanding what a huge deal this is. Don't worry about the "few" beers. It really was just two or three. It just hit me hard because I hadn't eaten dinner and had been running around delivering pizzas for a few hours.

I have to admit that I feel a little weird that you wrote a song about my "situation." I mean, on the one hand, it is incredibly touching and sweet, and I appreciate that you care so much, but on the other hand, I feel like it might be, I don't know, humiliating, in a way. I shouldn't jump to conclusions because I haven't read the lyrics or anything, but I'm just thinking about you singing it at the Morrisons' party over Thanksgiving, in front of everyone from our high school, and if it's *obvious* that it's about my family, that would be really uncomfortable. I don't know how to explain this, but this whole thing with my dad makes me feel like a real loser. Like I'm from "the wrong side of the tracks" all of a sudden. (Holy crap, when did I start overusing quotation marks? That's your "thing"!)

But you know what, screw it! It doesn't even matter. My mom just called to tell me that we're going to her sister's house in Virginia for Thanksgiving. As if my life could get ANY WORSE! She's picking me up here for the "short drive over the mountains." I'm dying. I won't get to see everyone. I won't get to see your band. I won't get to see Annie or Dee or Connie or Liz or Claire. So sing whatever you want at the party because I WON'T BE THERE!!!

And to top it off, my dad is going to "swing by" my aunt's (from where, I don't know) (and seriously, who "swings by" over the mountains?) to bring me back to school. Now THAT will be an awesome drive.

I'm going to throw up now.

Your extremely depressed friend,
Cath

P.S. Please tell me my name isn't in the song you wrote, like in the song with Samantha's name. "Here's a story that should make you wary / Cath's dad banged the secretary."

P.P.S. I don't really care about your thing with Dorothy. She's not the greatest roommate, but it's not like you're going to be living together. Or maybe you are. Who the hell knows anymore. But next time you visit and are going to hook up, take her to the stacks!

P.P.P.S. Of course your dad can beat up my dad. How much would he charge me to do it?

November 16, 1982

Cath,

Excuse me, but you're just figuring out now that we grew up on the "wrong side of the tracks"? Were you not paying attention for 18 years? Did something ever happen that suggested to you that we were on the "right side of the tracks"? Did you think the smell from the Candelaria's septic tank was the smell of the "right side of the tracks"? Did you think the kids on the "right side of the tracks" ate baloney sandwiches for dinner? With store-brand soda?

I'm kidding, at least a little. I think we grew up firmly in the middle of the tracks, just waiting for the train to hit us. Maybe it just did. (How's that for a metaphor, Mrs. Anki? Still think I deserved a D in sophomore English, you old bag of socks?)

There's nothing going on with me and Dorothy. And if there is, I still blame you 100%. Anyway, I don't think she's as bad as you think she is. I think she's just lonely and feeling out of place around a lot of very brainy people with very different backgrounds than hers. Maybe you could cut her a break. I think she really wants to be your friend.

The band practiced that new song I wrote, and I have to tell you that I really like it, as does the rest of the band. It's called "Daddy Issues," and it's an up-tempo number that is kind of at odds with the seriousness of the lyrics, sort of like what Elvis Costello does with some of his songs. You know how his songs are fast and almost poppy, but the lyrics can be very dark? Well, same thing here. Plus, I changed one of the lyrics a little to steal a phrase I liked from one of your letters. If you think I'm going to share songwriting credit with you, you're crazy.

Here are the lyrics, only because you asked for them. Let me know what you think.

> It started with a rumor,
> And it grew just like a tumor.
> That's the problem with a toybox town.
> Something happens and it gets around.
>
> They say your daddy he's been bad, bad, bad.
> And it makes your mommy so sad, sad, sad.
> Whisper, whisper, whisper, whisper.
> "Did you hear that he kissed her?"
>
> And what has that done to you?
> It makes you angry, it makes you blue.
> You've always been Daddy's best little girl.
> But when he lies, his lips begin to curl.
>
> (Chorus) So here's a Coke and a box of tissues.
> Congratulations, you have daddy issues.
> Daddy issues.

"Sorry, honey, I'll be working late.
I've got reports and a firm due date.
My secretary? Yes, she's here still.
She needs the overtime to pay her bills."

You feel their eyes when you walk through school.
As if you knew that girl in the typing pool.
The one they're saying grew up dirt poor,
And is showing him how to lock his office door.

(Chorus) So here's a Coke and a box of tissues.
Congratulations, you have daddy issues.
Daddy issues.

Mommy's turning on and off the lamp.
Daddy comes home and his hair is damp.
"I just washed up in the bathroom sink.
Sweating all day, didn't want to stink."

From the stairs you watch the world go south.
You see the curl at the corner of his mouth.
As he passes you, he tries to kiss you.
He doesn't know you have daddy issues.

(Chorus) So here's a Coke and a box of tissues.
Congratulations, you have daddy issues.
Daddy issues.

Things get better as time goes by.
But you know it's just lie, lie, lie.
What if you tell your mother what you know
About the guy who pays for your clothes.

And your food and the roof above your head,
Your record player and your queen-size bed.
You keep your mouth shut and pretend you don't know,
And now you're part of your father's show.

(Chorus) So here's a Coke and a box of tissues.
Congratulations, you have daddy issues.
Daddy issues.

I hope you like it. If not, let me know. Like I said, it just sort of came to me on the drive home after our visit. (It was originally called "Cath's Dad's a Super-Douche." As I think you can see, I toned it down a bit, mostly because there aren't a lot of words that rhyme with "super-douche.")

Also, I don't remember if I told you, but I'm not the lead guitarist anymore. Joe is. We switched and now I'm the rhythm guitarist, but I'm still singing the lead vocals. I'm cool with that. I have to admit that it was a little tricky trying to sing and play lead at the same time. Half the time I would forget to sing because I was concentrating so hard on the guitar part.

I'm sorry that you're not coming home for Thanksgiving. That sucks like a Hoover. (I'm working on my metaphors for our songs.) But I'm afraid I'm going to have to work most of that weekend anyway since it's the start of the Christmas shopping season. Maybe you can call me from your aunt's house.

Okay, I'm going to run. Looking forward to what you have to say about the new song. Sorry things suck so bad these days. They'll get better, I promise.

Scott

P.S. My dad will beat up your dad for free. Or "gratis," as they would say in Latin America.

P.P.S. Quote of the day from my dad: "Hey, Scott, do you know what's happening with all of our goddamn stationery? It's disappearing!" No, Dad, I have no idea where your stationery is going.

November 18, 1982

Cath,

Haven't heard back from you. Just checking to make sure you got my last letter, the one with the lyrics to the song I wrote and the offer to have my dad beat up your dad, no charge.

Maybe it got lost in the mail.

Or maybe you hated the song.

I'm betting on lost in the mail.

Scott

November 19, 1982

Cath?

Hello?
Is anyone there?
Is this microphone working?

Scott

Scott,

I'm sorry it's taken me a few days to write back to you and tell you
what I think of your new song. I guess I could lie and tell you I've
been too busy to write. But the truth is that I haven't been able to
figure out what I want to say.

Here's the thing, Scott. You know me as well as anyone, right?
And the first time I read your lyrics, I have to admit that I was pretty
hurt and pissed off. My first reaction was, "What an asshole! I can't
believe he thinks I knew my dad was cheating on my mom, or that I
hid it from her so my dad could buy me clothes! I thought he knew
me better than that! And I thought he had more respect for me than
that!"

But then I realized that, even though we are really good friends
and we know each other really well, it's hard to understand what it
feels like when your parents split up. I remember when Matt Mill-
er's parents got a divorce and he went from being like the smartest
kid in our class to smoking cigarettes and hanging out with the
fleabags outside the cafeteria at school, and I wanted to shake him
and say "Hey, man, knock it off! You're still really smart! Don't let
this fuck you up!" But now I know it's not that easy. Now I know
it'd probably be better to just sit next to him while he smokes his
cigarettes and tries to figure it out. And it's not about figuring out if
I knew my dad was cheating on my mom. I can honestly tell you
that it never even occurred to me that my dad was having an affair.

93

Even when my dad's secretary got pregnant and I overheard some-one whisper "Do you think Mr. Osteen did it?" I was like, "Yeah, right, my dad's *an accountant,* in case you didn't know." He's about as straight as a dad can be. I would have never, ever thought he would cheat on my mom. I mean, she loves my dad, and she's pretty and smart and upbeat and fun at parties and all that. She does everything for him. I mean, *everything.* She irons his shirts because he doesn't like the starch that the cleaners use. She runs our whole life around his work and the tax year. She makes special meals around quarterly filing dates. "Things that hold up well the next day in Tupperware so your dad doesn't have to walk out to lunch when he's so busy." And you know we could never take a regular spring break vacation. God forbid that a moment of spring before April 15 would be devoted to anything other than preparing random people's tax returns. Remember last year when she broke her wrist and called me at school rather than him at work because it was too close to a filing deadline?

I don't even know what I'm trying to figure out. Your lyrics stung pretty badly at first, but I'm hoping you don't really think those things about me. Maybe you were working with words to find rhymes and pacing or whatever, and hopefully our lunch conversa-tion didn't inspire all those specific thoughts. And maybe the song will be really different when I hear it set to music. Whatever, I'm sort of trying to make excuses because I really hope that's not how you think about me.

Not that I want you to write even more realistic song lyrics about this situation or anything, but I have spent a lot of time wondering if I contributed to my dad's decision to leave. Not because I suspected that he was having an affair and I didn't say anything, but just by, like, not being a better daughter. Like when I was first dating Todd and we were all hanging out at McDonald's way past curfew and when we got home my dad was getting in the car to go and look for me? He was so furious, he couldn't even talk to me until the next day. And all the times I rolled my eyes at things he said, or when I'd say "hardy-har-har" in a bitchy way when he tried to be funny, or when I'd just hang out in my room so I didn't have to deal with his questions about school and grades and SAT scores and college applications and whatever. Or that time at the breakfast table when he saw a hickey on my neck and he just got up and left for work without even saying good-bye. I mean, is it that kind of stuff? Is he just over trying to be a good dad to a kid who's not even going to be nice to him? Does he think I don't need a dad anymore? I feel like all that stuff is normal teenage stuff, but it also makes me cry with shame to think about how easy it would have been to be nicer to him. And now my mom is alone, and I feel pretty shitty about it all.

So, anyway, that's a long way of saying that I've been avoiding telling you what I think of your new song because I've been trying to figure things out. I haven't made much progress, and for some strange reason, I feel like smoking a cigarette outside the Pit, even though cigarettes are the grossest things in the world.

All of this is a long way of saying I don't know what I think of your song. Sorry.

Love,
Cath

P.S. While we're talking about gross stuff, you might call someone like my dad a "phony baloney," but the sandwich meat is actually spelled "bologna." And no. I'm not kidding.

November 22, 1982

Cath,

Whoa, whoa, whoa, whoa, whoa! Hold your horses.

First of all, the song isn't about you in particular. Your situation inspired the song, but it's not about you. And you're right that some of the lyrics are just there because I had to make the song longer or because they rhymed.

Second, it's a song. That's it. It's not meant to be anything more than that.

Third, I don't think you knew anything was going on with your dad and his secretary, and you know that. How many conversations did we have about those rumors last summer before you ran off to college? A million? Did I ever say anything to you suggesting that I thought you knew something was going on with your dad and that skank? No. Did I agree with you every single time you said that it was impossible for something to be going on with them? Yes.

Fourth, do you remember about a week before you left for college, you got all sentimental and told me that I'm your best friend, and I didn't say it back? And remember how we hardly saw each other that last week because I had to work and we didn't really say good-bye before you left? Have you figured out why that was, college girl? It's because I was afraid I might start crying if we actually said good-bye. I didn't want to think about what it was going to be like not to have you around anymore. (It sucks, in case you were wondering.) And I don't really feel like talking about it now, either. But if you believe I think you're a terrible person, you're out of your mind. You're one of the best people I know. You're funny, smart, incredibly good-looking even if you don't think so, and nice to dogs and neighbors. And I will deny writing this paragraph if you ever bring it up, particularly the part about you being good-looking.

I would never want to hurt you, Cath, and I'm sorry that this has made you so upset. So I am retiring "Daddy Issues." I'm throwing it away. No big deal. I'll just write some different lyrics to go with the music. I can call it "Facial Tissues"!

Scott

P.S. I didn't say I was afraid I'd cry. You must have misread that.

WAKE FOREST
UNIVERSITY

Scott,

Thank you for your letter and for not telling me you were afraid you'd cry.

Thanks for all the kind words. And for confirming you didn't think I knew about my dad. That means a lot to me.

And thank you for admitting you think I'm good-looking. It's mutual. (I don't mean that I also think that I'm good-looking, but I think you are. And I'll deny that, too, if you ever tell anyone.)

I went back and reread "Daddy Issues" after getting your letter. I hope you don't mind, but I showed it to Jane down the hall, too, and her response was, "That's fucking amazing." She helped me not to take it so personally. We all know kids whose parents are divorced, right? And the lyrics are good, Scott. Really good. They're powerful. (And did I mention that it's also ridiculous that you got me to do your English homework for four years when you can write something like that?! You are a total scam artist!) Anyway, please don't throw the song away. You should play it. Maybe just not when I'm around.

And speaking of rock stars, I finally have something fun to tell you about. My manager at the Pizza Pan also works for the university productions department, and he got me a job as an usher at the Joe Jackson concert last night! It was totally out of the blue. He had someone cancel on him at the last minute, and my training consisted of putting on a blue vest and carrying a flashlight. It's actually kind of funny how much authority a blue vest and a flashlight will give you. My job was to remind people not to dance in the aisles, which was easy to achieve because I was paired up with a football player.

Anyway, I don't know much about Joe Jackson—I know he did that song called "Is She Really Going Out with Him?" but that's about it. (And I only know that because you would sing it whenever you saw me with Todd. Always Mr. Subtle.) Anyway, everyone was really psyched to have a great time. And then Joe Jackson came onstage and basically started playing a piano recital. His first song was—and I kid you not—about *cancer*. Yes, cancer. The chorus went, "Everything gives you cancer." He kept repeating that over and over again. "Everything. Everything gives you cancer. Everything." You get the point. And it was not up-tempo. Not at all. Talk about a buzz-kill! People started walking around, talking and chatting, anything to escape the dismal cancer song. And then Joe Jackson STOPPED. He stopped playing and told the audience to pay attention. Excuse me? You come to a college campus and are a complete downer and then call the audience rude? It did eventually get better—but, man, *that* was a terrible start to a concert. I kept thinking, "Remember to tell Scott not to sing about cancer, and not to yell at the crowd, and he'll be a lot more fun than Joe Jackson."

So don't sing about cancer, okay? But please do play "Daddy Issues." I am so sorry that I'll miss your big concert. I would love to be there to support you. I know you guys will be GREAT, and I can't wait to hear all about it. And you have to tell me about everyone from high school and who hooked up or got drunk or thinks they are super cool now that they're in college, or whatever. I know it will be a hugely busy weekend for you with the party and the after-Thanksgiving sales. I'll call you from my aunt's house. Don't leave out any details!

Love,
Cath

P.S. While you shouldn't sing about cancer, you might want to think about hepatitis. If you rhyme it with "encephalitis," and throw in a dose of syphilis, that might be a Top 10 hit.

P.P.S. Be cool when you see Samantha, okay?

P.P.P.S. I would've cried, too, you moron. And I would have loved every second of it.

November 24, 1982

Cath—

The song is retired. Gone. Good-bye. Adios. However you say "good-bye" in French. It's done. I'm already working on some new lyrics for it.

Case closed.

We're going to mostly play cover songs at the party anyway. We have some great stuff lined up—everything from the Beatles to Bruce Springsteen to the Cars. We may play that "Samantha Drew" song, though. I took your advice and changed the name to "Jeanie Blue" so Samantha won't think I've been sitting at home all this time just thinking about her. And I'm not doing that. Anymore. As far as you know. (In fact, I have a great deal of evidence to prove that I'm not spending all my time thinking about her, and that I'm spending WAY too much of my time swapping letters with some other girl at Wake Forest.)

Have a great Thanksgiving with your mom and your aunt. Give me a call when you get a chance. Just not during the football game, okay? And not when we're playing at the party. And not Friday, Saturday, or Sunday when I'm at the store.

Scott

P.S. Hey, how's Dorothy doing?

Dear Scott,

It's Thanksgiving night. I didn't get another letter from you before we drove here, and your phone has been busy every time I've tried to call.

I hope you and your family had a nice Thanksgiving. And I hope the party went really well last night. I especially hope that everyone loved your "Daddy Issues" song.

This time at my aunt's house has been so hard. My mom looks about 10 years older than she did just a few months ago. Somehow she's both gaunt and puffy at the same time, if you can imagine that. It's like her face is a different shape or something. And she's trying so hard. Everyone is trying so hard. To be happy. To be cheerful. To be thankful. For something. Anything. It all feels fake and forced.

So I basically shut down. At dinner, I couldn't bring myself to speak. To add to the awkwardness. It was all I could do NOT to speak. Not to say the things I really wanted to say. Like—

"My dad's supposed to be at the head of the table."

"You're not supposed to carve the turkey in the kitchen. You're supposed to make a big show of carving it at the table. My dad is supposed to carve the turkey. At the head of the table. And make the plates. And he knows not to put gravy on my stuffing. Only on my potatoes. Why did you put gravy on my stuffing?"

"My mother doesn't drink vodka at the table."

"This turkey is cold. And dry. But Plum likes it."

"No, it's not about time for 'another round.' "

"Stop asking if I want MORE. You are supposed to know what I need and say 'Just another smidge to even things out.' "

"Do not put *that* on my plate."

"Plum is going to have stomachache."

"Stop laughing like that. It's not funny. Nothing you are saying is funny."

"Dear God, please make them stop."

"My family doesn't act like this."

"We don't get drunk on Thanksgiving."

"We don't go from cackling to crying before the dessert plates are cleared."

"We don't get tucked into bed at 5 in the afternoon."

"We don't wake up and pretend that nothing happened."

"My family does not do these things."

Love,
Cath

November 29, 1982

Cath,

Sorry we didn't get a chance to talk at all over Thanksgiving weekend. My mom said you called while I was at work on Friday and that she had a nice talk with you.

We played at the party on Wednesday night. It was a disaster. Oh, we sounded great. It's just that no one wanted to listen to us. Everyone was too busy talking and catching up. It was like we weren't even there. And Samantha showed up with her college boyfriend. She didn't say a word to me. Seriously, not a word. She just sort of nodded at me while I was singing, then turned her back on us for the entire night. I dated her for more than a year, and all I got was a head nod. The hell with her. And I'm glad I changed the name in that song. You were right, she doesn't deserve to have a song written about her.

Thanksgiving Day was fine. I won't bore you with the details—turkey, stuffing, my dad falling asleep on the couch watching the football game. Nothing special.

Then I had to work 12-hour shifts on Friday, Saturday, and Sunday. I've never seen the store so busy, and I was wiped out by the time we got home Sunday night. The stuff that we put on sale is all the stuff from the summer and fall that we hadn't sold yet, so we were just happy to get it out of the store, but you'd think we were giving away free money all weekend. There wasn't a moment when I wasn't helping at least one customer. It was

105

crazy, just crazy, but kind of exciting. And my dad couldn't stop smiling. On the drive home Sunday night, he slipped me a hundred-dollar bill and said, "Don't tell your mother." As if my mother would care. Anyway, I am now a very rich man. I have a hundred-dollar bill in my wallet. It has a picture of Benjamin Franklin on it, if you don't believe me. He was the President once, I believe. Or maybe he was the King of England.

Okay, I don't want this to be weird, but do you know what's going on with Dorothy? Did she go home for Thanksgiving? I tried to call her to wish her a happy Thanksgiving, but some girl in your dorm said she'd left already for the holiday. Please tell her I tried to call, okay?

On a different note, a lot of people asked about you over the weekend, and everybody says hello. I might have told a few of them that you dropped out of college to join the rodeo. And a few of them might have thought I was being serious. So next time you come home, it would be great if you could arrive on a horse. And please wear chaps. Let me know if you need help ordering a pair.

Let's talk soon.

Scott

P.S. If I ever mention Samantha again, I want you to come home and hit me over the head with something heavy. An anvil should work, if you happen to have one. If not, I think Acme

Products sells them. At least that's where the Coyote always seems to go to purchase his anvils in the Road Runner cartoons.

P.P.S. I don't want to sound like a narc, but your dad stopped by your house on Thanksgiving Day with his pregnant skank of a secretary and took the big TV set that you had in your living room. We watched him from the living room window while he was sneaking around. What a douche. Someone should write a song about him.

P.P.P.S. I'm joking. About the song, not about the TV. Or about your dad being a super-douche.

Dear Scott,

It's Monday, and I'm back at school. I'm sorry we never got a chance to talk over Thanksgiving weekend. It was great to talk to your mom, though. I really missed coming over on Thanksgiving morning and helping her slice the apples for her pies. She's such a sweet lady.

I wanted to write again because my last letter was such a downer. I'm sorry about that. It was a hard day, but things got much better after that. The weather was perfect and I went for some long runs with Plum. (Did I mention that I *love* that dog?) We braved the crowds and went to the mall yesterday, which was wild. I thought about you and your dad stuck at the store all weekend. I hope it went well. My mother can work a shopping mall like nobody's business. She has it down to a science. Her sister is equally impressive. Together, they are a retail force to be reckoned with, let me tell you.

And we did some of my favorite mom's-side-of-the-family stuff. We sat by the fire and played backgammon and cribbage and hearts. We found an old jigsaw puzzle and my mom and her sister sang Tom Jones songs. ("What's new, pussycat? Whoa, whoa, whoa.") It was actually pretty fun. But when it was my turn to sing, the only song I could think of was that Joe Jackson song about cancer. I'm not kidding. And the harder I tried to think of another song, the only song I could think about was the cancer song. And then I couldn't stop myself from singing it. Yikes! Fortunately, everyone just thought I was trying to be funny, and I ended up telling them about what happened at the concert, and before you knew it, everyone was swapping funny stories about the things that have happened at concerts they went to. It was great!

My mom was right to bring us there. Thanksgiving was hard, but it would have been much worse at home. After dominating the household in backgammon—I rock!—I almost felt ready to drive back to school with my dad on Sunday. But I was wrong about that. In a word, it was brutal. Or perhaps I should say that it had its ups and downs. You decide.

First, my aunt insisted on fixing me a big Sunday morning breakfast. (Corned beef hash and a fried egg, in case you're keeping track.) My dad showed up right as I was finishing, and my aunt said to me, "You just sit right there." She opened the door, let the dog out, told my dad that I'll be out as soon as I finish my breakfast, and slammed the door in his face. I could see him through the picture window as Plum gave him a complete proctological exam and rubbed blond fur all over my dad's pants. (Have I mentioned that I *love* that dog?) Plum trailed him to the car and started barking up a storm. And then I saw it. It's a *new* car. It's a big, black Mercedes-Benz. My mom is going to lose her mind! She's a nervous wreck about money, and he buys himself a Mercedes? I ran upstairs to hug her good-bye so she wouldn't look out the window, and then I went outside. My dad gave me a hug like nothing was wrong and gave me that "little princess" nonsense again, then took my bag to the car. The dog was still going crazy, mostly on the passenger side of the car, and then I saw what looked like a big fluffy cat in the car. Only it wasn't a cat. It was the Slutty Secretary with the biggest hairdo you've ever seen! I couldn't believe it. I was not ready for that. I was *really* not ready for that.

She said, "Cath-LEEN, it's so nice to see you again!"

My dad said, "No no, sweetie, her name is Catherine."

She said, "I'm so silly!"

My brain said, "I think you mean 'stupid.' You're so stupid."

All the while, Plum was still barking, and my dad was trying to get the car in gear. (Did I mention it's a stick shift? He doesn't even know how to drive a stick shift!) He finally got it into reverse and popped the clutch so hard that I flew forward and smashed my nose on the back of the seat.

He laughed and said, "And we're off!"

She said, "Now, honey, don't bleed on the seat. It's *real leather.*"

That's when I realized my nose was bleeding, not a lot, just a little. I tipped my head back and felt the blood drip down my throat. It was sort of a relief to have to breathe through my mouth because I think she put on her perfume with a ladle. Or a fire hose.

And then she started touching him. She was trying to brush the dog fur off his shiny black pants. (There's no way he bought them at your dad's store. They're way too tacky.) She was turned sideways in her seat and was swatting at his pants and saying stupid things like "That's right," or "Yes, indeedy," or "You got that right, buster!" while she stroked his leg or tapped him on the shoulder. Tap tap tap.

But nothing he was saying was right, and he was definitely not driving right as we went herkety-jerkety up the mountain.

He said, "I want us all to be friends."

My brain said, "You're my dad. You're not my friend. And she's definitely not my friend."

He said, "I know it's hard, but you're old enough to handle it."

My brain said, "Old enough? My mother's almost 50 and she's not even old enough to handle this. Have you seen her lately, by the way? You know, your WIFE."

He said, "Besides, you always wanted a little brother or sister!"

My brain said, "You talked me out of that, remember? You told me I was your princess. I was the only princess you needed."

He said, "Blah blah blah" about "financial arrangements" and "settlements" and "your mother really doesn't need a lawyer" and a bunch of accounting stuff that I just couldn't follow because my brain was saying, "Jesus Christ, lady, would you stop touching him, already?"

I was breathing through my nose again and the perfume was killing me, so I said, "Could you please open the window?"

She tapped him (again!) and mouthed, "My hair."

So he wouldn't open the window even though, clearly, she could ride the whole way home with her head stuck out of the window and nothing would put a dent in that bird's nest.

And then, for some reason, my dad started talking about their "relationship." He said that "Whew, it just snuck up on us and well, unfortunately, we fell in love."

She said, "Yep, we fell in love." Stroke stroke stroke.

My brain said, "I don't think 'unfortunately' is the right word there."

He said, "Blah blah blah, blah blah, blah blah."

And I kept thinking, "Unfortunately? Really?"

He was still struggling with the car, trying to find the right gear for going down the mountain. He was coasting and then popping the clutch, and the engine was screaming and she decided it was a good time to talk about food.

She said, "Do they feed you anything at that school of yours? You're kind of skinny. I hope you're not paying for a big meal plan. Ha ha ha!"

I said, "I'm skinny because I run."

My brain added, "And because I can't eat thinking about you sleeping with my dad." [It's possible that my brain may have concluded with a nasty insult, something along the lines of "you stupid slut-faced bitch," but I can't swear by it, because I started crying and things went a little sideways at that point.]

The crying made my nose bleed again, and I tried to tip my head back, but between the crying and the perfume and car jerking along, well, I threw up. Yep. I vomited all over the backseat of my dad's new Mercedes-Benz.

He said, "Oh, Catherine."

I said, "Whew. Unfortunately, that just snuck up on me."

We had to pull over and try to clean up the mess using one of the sweatshirts that was in my bag. We had to keep the windows

112

open the rest of the drive, and we didn't talk at all. Needless to say, he didn't give me a kiss good-bye when we arrived at school. I just mumbled something about needing to start studying for finals and walked away. And to tell you the truth, I'm a bit worried that my head is not in a "final exams" type of place right now.

Well, I'm exhausted, how about you? It was a long story, but admit it, you're kind of proud of me right now.

I can't wait to hear about YOUR weekend! Please tell me something fun!

Your very curious friend,
Cath

P.S. There was a note on our door from Cindy down the hall saying that you called to wish Dorothy a Happy Thanksgiving. She was really happy when she got it. I don't know what's going on with you two, but I'm sorry that I've been mean about her. I've been joking. Mostly. The nightly pizzas *were* a total, smelly drag. You gotta give me that one. But I actually sort of missed the snoring while at my aunt's house. I should make a tape recording of Dorothy snoring to listen to when she's not around. It helps me sleep. Go figure.

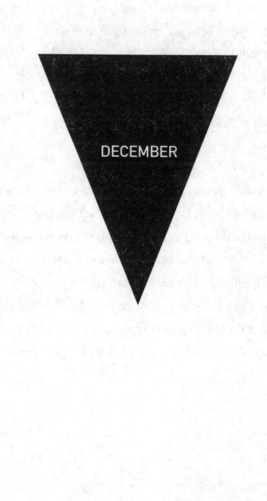

DECEMBER

December 1, 1982

Cath,

Okay, *that* was a long letter. That's the longest thing I've read since I read *Middlemarch* junior year. Or, more accurately, since I read the Cliff's Notes to *Middlemarch* junior year. But even the Cliff's Notes were long.

I don't know what to say in response to your letter. I mean, the whole thing sucks, and it sounds horrible, but I don't know what to say other than that. The part where you threw up in your dad's car was funny, but the rest of it just sounds terrible. Whatever else you would like me to say, can we just assume that I actually said it? And can we also assume that I called your dad a super-douche exactly as often as I should in response to that story? I know this is important to you, and I don't want to say the wrong thing. And I don't want to say too much or not enough. Okay?

If it makes you feel any better, I lied to you about Thanksgiving. It was horrible, but I just didn't feel like telling you. The party may have been the worst night of my life. Everyone was home from college. They were all wearing their college sweatshirts, and they'd all brought their new college boyfriends or girlfriends home for the weekend. And they were all shrieking when they first saw each other, and hugging each other because they hadn't seen each other in months. Well, I grew up with all of them, I went to high school with all of them, and they hadn't

115

seen me for just as long. But no one shrieked when they saw me, and no one came over to hug me.

No one. Literally, no one. The most anyone could do was to nod in my direction, and not many of them did that.

They made it very clear that I'm just the guy from the clothing store now. I'm just the guy in the band. All these people that I grew up with, that I went to school with, that I played baseball with, that I went to parties with and hung out with after school—they're all better than me now. Just because I don't have a fucking college sweatshirt. I hate them all, Cath. I hate every last one of them. I hadn't been feeling like a complete loser lately, but I do now.

As if that weren't bad enough, we then had to try to entertain them. But no one was listening to us. We might as well have been Muzak playing in an elevator. They had their backs to us and were talking the whole time, and no one seemed to notice when we would take a break. And when we did take a break, we stood off by ourselves and no one talked with us.

Samantha was there with her college boyfriend. They were both wearing their college sweatshirts. I thought she would at least come over to say hello, maybe bring him over and introduce us so we could all pretend to be adults, but all she did was nod once in my direction and that was it. After all that time together, all I got was a nod. And then it hit me what was going on—she didn't want to tell him that I used to be her boyfriend! She was too embarrassed to tell him that she used to date the guy in the band!

If you've heard from anyone from school, you may have already heard what happened next. But let me give you my version of it, okay? We were all getting pissed off that no one was listening to us play, and Joe just wanted to leave. But Todd and I said no, and we kept playing. And we sounded really good. But because no one was listening, we decided to stop playing covers and just play some of our own songs. We started with that song that originally had Samantha's name in it. I'd changed it from "Sometimes, Samantha Drew" to "Sometimes, Jeanie Blue." But when I got to the chorus, I accidentally started singing "Samantha Drew" instead of "Jeanie Blue." And it ended up that at least a few people were listening because, before you knew it, everyone had turned around and was listening to us. They were listening to me singing, "Sometimes, Samantha Drew, do you think of me / I know, Samantha Drew, that I think of you."

I thought they were enjoying it, so I kept going. But as soon as the song was over, they all started laughing. Everyone. Including Samantha and her boyfriend. It was horrible.

I just put my head down and walked out with my guitar and waited for the rest of the band by Todd's van. We left the drums and amps there, and Todd picked them up later.

If anyone tells you I was crying when I left, they're lying. It's a lie. I felt like a complete idiot, but I wasn't crying. I swear.

All weekend, our old classmates came into the store to buy clothes before going back to college. None of them even called me by name, or introduced me to their girlfriends, or asked how

I was doing. None of them. I had to wait on them and act like we were strangers, like we hadn't grown up together and hadn't gone to the same parties just six months ago. That's right, Stan Meara, we don't know each other. I didn't play Little League with you forever, and I certainly didn't sit next to you in Spanish class for three years. And you're right, Billy Donovan, we don't know each other, either. We weren't in the same Cub Scout troop, and our families didn't go on a camping trip together when we were 12. No, that must have been someone else named Billy Donovan who just happened to look exactly like you, you little motherfucker. Here, let me help you find some new Levi's. Here, let me measure your waist and inseam. Have a nice day, guy who doesn't know me, and thanks for shopping at Agee's.

Thank God for Crush. They might not be the greatest guys in the world, and we might not be the greatest band in the world, but at least they call me by my name and aren't ashamed to know me.

So, that's a long way of saying my Thanksgiving sucked.

Let's talk soon.

From,
The guy from the clothing store,
The guy in the band

P.S. I am no longer a Tornado.

December 3, 1982

Dear Scott,

I'm really, really sorry to hear about how you were treated by our
classmates over Thanksgiving. The part about them not really listening while you were playing at the party didn't sound that bad, at
first. I mean, I could see how they would be all excited about seeing each other and sort of treating the band like background music,
but it was very uncool of people not to even say hi to you guys. And
the part about Samantha. Oh, Scott, I'm just sorry that I wasn't there
to slap her stupid face. I know you guys had a pretty solid thing senior year, but I have *never* liked her. Not one bit! You know that.
She's totally self-centered and arrogant, and she gets away with it
because she's pretty and wears tight shirts. She probably hadn't even
told her new boyfriend that she dated you for a long time and then
was surprised by the song. Not that there's any excuse for her acting
like that. What a bitch. She makes me furious.

Oh, and by the way, you have a college girlfriend, too, if anyone cared to ask. Dorothy fell for you like a ton of bricks the first
time she laid eyes on you, so Samantha can stop thinking that she's
the center of the universe now.

Speaking of Dorothy, she came home from Thanksgiving with
a copy of the new Michael Jackson album. It's called *Thriller*, and it's
amazing with a capital *A*. The best song on it is called "Billie Jean."
How do I know it's the best song? Because Dorothy played it 50 times
in a row, and I still wasn't tired of it. You need to check it out.

Anyway, back to Thanksgiving weekend. Who came by the store over the weekend? Was it just Stan and Billy, or where there a lot of guys? Stan and Billy are sort of dorky guys, but I'm really surprised that they didn't even give you a "Hey, dude, what's going on?" I guess you have to expect a little awkwardness, especially if you're measuring their inseams or whatever—aren't you up in their business for that? But none of them even tried to be nice, at all? Man, Scott, I feel so bad. I don't want you to feel like a loser. You're such a great guy. You are. I'm not just saying that to try to make you feel better. You've always been the first person to watch out for me, to sit with me on the bus after a bad day, to talk to me when I was standing by myself at a middle school dance. You are always taking care of other people. I hate the thought of you being treated badly.

I'm really glad that you have your band. Todd might not be the best at putting things into words, but he will always have your back. And Joe's always been a good dude. (I don't know about the other guy, but I'll assume he's cool, too, until I see evidence to the contrary.)

I have to run to a review session for exams. I'm trying so hard to focus and it's not easy with my mom in hysterics over my father's shenanigans—she was NOT happy about the TV, let me tell you—or with the lyrics to "Billie Jean" swimming around in my head. ("Billie Jean is not my lover / She's just a girl who says that I am the one.")

Anyway, take care, best friend. Keep your head up and keep

writing songs. There's a lot more to you than selling clothes (even if that is an honorable profession and nothing to be ashamed of!).

Give my love to your mom and dad, and I'll tell your college girlfriend that you said hello.

Much love,
Cath

P.S. Not to sound too much like Donnie Dibsie, but you'll always be a Tornado, Scott. You couldn't change that now if you tried.

December 6, 1982

Dear Cath—

I hope this doesn't sound strange, but I had nothing to do tonight and ended up rereading a few of the letters you sent me a few months back. Remember when you called me "underachiever guy"? I've been trying to figure out what that means and how it happened. My dad was always on me about studying and trying to get good grades so I could go to college. That was his big thing, that he wanted me to be the first person in our family to get a college degree. So what did I do? I didn't study, I didn't get good grades, and I didn't go to college. I didn't even take the SAT exams. Now I'm thinking that maybe I went out of my way not to do what he wanted me to do. Do you think that's what I did? Why would I do that? It makes no sense. It's like I went out of my way to make a point to him, but I don't know what the hell the point was, and now I've screwed up my life. (Hey, maybe *I'm* the one with "daddy issues." How funny is that?) I screwed up my life to make a point to my dad, and I'm not even smart enough to know what the point was. And my dad's a good guy. He fought for his country, he works hard to provide for his family. Why wouldn't I want to do well in school if that was important to him? Why wouldn't I want to make him proud of me?

Maybe you should run that last paragraph by your psychology class. They teach you about things like that, don't they?

And whatever the answer is, please let me know so I can dwell on it for the next 50 years as I sell clothes to people who pretend they don't know me.

By the way, it wasn't just Stan and Billy who came into the store over Thanksgiving weekend. It was 5 or 6 guys, and they all acted the same—Mark, Danny, Bob, Pete, J.J. I don't think I mentioned this, but they didn't say hello to my dad either, even though they've known him for years, too. My dad was either their Little League coach or the den leader for their Cub Scout troop, but none of them even said hello to him. The weird thing about it is that it didn't bother him. I asked him about it a few days later when the store was quiet and we were just hanging out, and he didn't say much more to me than, "You can't ever let anything a teenager does bother you, because they don't know what the hell they're doing."

Anyway, I'm fine. I really am. I decided to write a song about what happened. It's called "You Don't Know Me." The lyrics are a little rough still, but I hope you'll think it's at least a good start:

> As boys we played on the playground seesaw,
> We went to parties in our teens.
> Unlike you, the only A's I ever saw,
> Was dressed as Fonzie on Halloween.
> Your grades have taken you away from our town,
> You're in college, ain't that nice.

And me, no choice but to stick around.
I took our guidance counselor's advice.

"Young man," he said 'cause he didn't know my name,
"The smart ones, they all go away.
And guys like you, well, it's a damn shame.
Guys like you they have to stay,
And get a job at the supermarket,
Maybe the car wash by the mall."
"Here's my Vette, be careful where you park it.
And shine it up with Armor All."

Me, I'm just the guy at the gasoline station,
Me, I'm just the singer in this band.
I wasn't asking you to make a donation,
I just thought you'd shake my hand.
But now it seems that you don't know me,
You don't know me
Anymore.

When we were six we were both Cub Scouts,
And we were both in the same troop.
We went camping and we each caught brook trout,
And our dads made brook trout soup.
When we were ten we both played baseball,

I played second, you played short.
When we were twelve we turned to football.
At fourteen, we said good-bye to sports.

Now I'm just the guy at the gasoline station,
Now I'm just the singer in this band.
Don't say what happened was an aberration,
That I just don't understand.
I understand that you don't know me,
You don't know me
Anymore.

You hear our song on the radio station,
"Hey, I know the singer in the band!"
Maybe it's getting played on heavy rotation,
Maybe we're on American Bandstand.
You can get on your feet and cheer us,
You can get down on your knees,
You can stand real close so you can hear us,
You can yell, "Look here, please!"

But I'm just the guy at the gasoline station,
And I'm just a singer in this band.
And this song, if it's sweeping the nation,
I'll bet you still won't understand,

If I say that I don't know you.
I don't know you
Anymore.

I think I used the word "aberration" right. And I think I spelled it right, too. If not, please let me know.

On a different note, I don't think you should call Dorothy my "girlfriend." I haven't even called her that yet.

And on another different note, I've heard *Thriller*, and I agree that it's great. The radio station's been playing one of the songs on it called "Wanna Be Startin' Somethin'." Hand on Bible, I thought he was singing, "Wanna Be Donna Summer." ("Wanna be Donna Summer / Gotta be Donna Summer.") Either way, it's a great song. I could see us dancing to that. Maybe you could even take a picture of me dancing to it. (Sorry, but I was thinking of that letter where you said you could prove I liked Tony Orlando and Dawn because you have a picture of me dancing to it. I'm still waiting for you to explain that to me, college girl!)

Good luck with your final exams.

Scott

P.S. Your mom and my mom went to the mall together today. Wait until you see what you're getting for Christmas! I'm laughing my ass off just thinking about it. I'm not going to tell you what it is, but you'd better pray your mom keeps the receipt.

P.P.S. We're playing at Duffy's tomorrow night. If we can set up the tape recorder, I'll send you a tape.

P.P.P.S. Ha! Ha! Ha! Ha! Ha! Ha! Ha! Ha! Ha! Ha! Ha! Ha! Ha! Ha! Ha! Ha! Ha! Ha! (Sorry, but I was just thinking about your Christmas present.)

December 8, 1982

Dear Cath,

Here's the tape from Duffy's last night. The quality's not great because you can hear one of the waitresses standing by the tape recorder talking.

But you will still be able to tell that we rocked!

We TOTALLY ROCKED!

Let me know what you think, but if you reach any conclusion other than that we TOTALLY ROCKED, then there's something seriously wrong with you! Why? Because we TOTALLY ROCKED!

Scott

P.S. Ha! Ha! Ha! Ha! Ha! Ha! Ha! Ha! Ha! Ha! Ha! Ha! Ha! Ha! Ha! Ha! Ha! Ha! (Sorry, but I was just thinking about your Christmas present again.)

December 8, 1982

Dear Scott,

I have to start by telling you about the study guide that Jane made for me that is supposed to rule my life for the next few weeks. She helped me make a chart for the finals reading and exam period with blocks of time color-coded on each day to indicate which subject I should study during which block of time. (I know, I know, I'm a huge nerd, but calling me that during finals would be a compliment, so go for it!)

I tell you that because I am writing to you during the last part of a GREEN time block, which is reserved for Psych 101. And don't feel bad about cutting into my study time, because I am feeling slightly cocky about my Psych exam. I like the class and, even with everything else going on in my life, or maybe because of everything else going on in my life, I've been able to concentrate in that particular class. I've taken really good notes all semester, which over the past few GREEN periods, I have rewritten and organized to go along with the textbook, so I think I am in good shape.

But I digress! And I apologize if I've had too many cans of Tab and am a little hyper. Caffeinated soda has become my close friend here at college, especially during FINALS. Our fridge is like an Andy Warhol painting of Tab cans. Anyway, the point here is that we are psychoanalyzing you during some extra time at the end of a GREEN period, leading into a block of calming BLUE downtime.

Keeping in mind that Psych 101 is a very introductory class and not a more high-level class like Abnormal Psych (clearly applicable to you), or Freudian Analysis (probably applicable to you), or The Crippling Effects of Daddy Issues (okay, so maybe that isn't really a class, but it would be so applicable to both me and you), I am going to take a shot at using it to address your "underachiever guy" question. One thing we've talked about in class is the nature–nurture debate. There are different schools of thought on how much a person's development is influenced by their natural genetic makeup and how much they are molded and nurtured by environmental influences. Some scholars say we are purely the product of our nature, some say that we are purely the result of environmental influences, and some say we are a mix of both. The "underachiever guy" thing can be analyzed under those schools of thought. On the nature side of things, I could say that you are following in your dad's footsteps because you are genetically very similar to him and, like him, despite being a very smart, sensitive, caring guy, you didn't get great grades, didn't go to college, and are now a salesman. On the nurturing side of things, I could say that you didn't go to college because your dad put way too much pressure on you and, like a lot of teenagers, you hated being told what to do and you reacted by doing just the opposite. As your friend, I would say it was probably a mix of those natural and environmental things, plus a bunch of other stuff, like being a funny guy who liked to make everyone laugh by clowning around in class, dating the very high-maintenance Samantha during senior year (seriously, she could have killed Larry

Varella's GPA), and obsessing over learning all the guitar parts of the Pretenders' first album.

The most important thing, though, is that you haven't screwed up your life. You could still go to college if you really wanted to. But I'm feeling like that's not what you want to do, anyway. You're hitting your stride with these great songs that you are writing. You are really talented, Scott. Please send me a tape of Crush performing your original songs. I really want to hear the lyrics paired with the music, including "Daddy Issues" (I'm sorry I was so Everything-Is-About-Me about that song—I really do want to hear it) and "You Don't Know Me." I'm a little worried about how I will react to the Samantha song after what you told me about the party, but send it anyway, okay? Would it be okay if Jane, Dorothy, and I all listen to the tape when you send it? I know they will want to hear Crush, and it would be a fun and distracting thing for us to do during one of our BLUE periods.

Okay, I've got to get going. My mother called during my last YELLOW period and I had to talk to her for most of it, so now I am even more behind on Biology than before. (Of course, Biology is YELLOW, as in "You might want to start paying attention to this, RIGHT NOW!") Unfortunately, my mom saw the S.S. Secretary and my dad steaming up and down the aisles in the grocery store and it was very upsetting for her. She was also nervous and excited because she got a part-time job at the card store for the holidays. Obviously, my mom is having her ups and downs, but I'm hopeful that getting out of the house and going back to work will be really good for her.

Okay, now I've really gotta go.

Waiting for my rocker friend's tape,
College Girl

P.S. I won't call Dorothy your "girlfriend" if you won't call James my "College Boyfriend Number 2." Or anything else with the phrase "Number 2" in it.

P.P.S. Sorry I missed your call the other night, although Dorothy seemed quite happy to have talked to you. I'm wondering who you were really calling to talk to in the first place—not-your-girlfriend-Dorothy or your friend who happens to be a girl, Cath?

P.P.P.S. I'm not tired of "Billie Jean" yet, even though not-your-girlfriend-Dorothy has played it at least 500 times since I last wrote. And I'm not exaggerating. But here's the thing. She's changed the lyrics when she sings along. What does she sing? "Scott Agee is now my boyfriend / He's just a boy who thinks that I am the one / Someday we'll have a son." Yup, she not only considers you her boyfriend, but she's already singing about having a child with you! You're still going to name him little Disease Ridden Genitals Agee, right?

P.P.P.P.S. I can't even think about Christmas right now, but I'm glad you're getting such a kick out of my present. Perhaps I should just plan on wrapping it back up and giving it to you since it obviously brings you so much joy!

December 11, 1982

Dear Cath,

Our letters must have crossed in the mail again because by the time I got your letter, I was already in a great mood. In case you haven't already heard, we TOTALLY ROCKED at Duffy's last week. Did you listen to the tape? Did you hear the crowd? They loved us. They totally loved us. And did you hear how they reacted to "You Don't Know Me"? Did you *hear* that? I don't care that they were drunk off their asses. They were singing along to a song I wrote and I sang. I've been on Cloud Eleven ever since. (Sorry, but Cloud Nine is for losers. And Cloud Ten is under construction.)

Enough talking about how great I am. Let's talk about *you* for a moment, okay? How great do *you* think I am? I don't mean to put you on the spot, but you must feel awfully warm right now. I mean, basking in my glory and everything.

We have three more gigs lined up before Christmas, including one at the Cat's Eye Pub in Baltimore, and we may end up with a regular gig at Duffy's on Thursday nights, which would be pretty cool. We're having some stickers made up with the band's logo on them to give out. Joe's sister designed it, and it looks pretty awesome. We figure if people start seeing the stickers around town, they might want to come check us out when we play. And what happens when we play? We rock! We

TOTALLY ROCK! But I didn't need to tell you that, because you already heard the tape and know we rock.

Okay, I'll stop talking about myself. For a moment.

Dorothy told me about James. She said he's a much nicer guy than Walter. I'm glad to hear that. But I'm still happy to beat the crap out of Walter the next time I come down, just for the exercise. (I'm joking, of course. I can't get into fights now. The last thing I need is for someone to punch me in the mouth. After all, my mouth is now my money-maker, baby!)

Oh, I'm sorry, I'm talking about myself again. Seriously, let's talk about you. So I'm glad to hear about James. And I'm glad that you, Dorothy, and Jane are having fun preparing for your final exams. I still think the best way to study is to wait until the bus ride to school in the morning, but I suppose you three would know better. Plus, they don't even have buses at your school, do they? How cheap of them.

Thank you for all your thoughts about my life. I really appreciate it. It's funny that you suggested applying to colleges because I was already thinking about doing that. But then something happened—I BECAME A ROCK STAR. So I'm not thinking about that anymore.

I'm glad to hear your mom got a job at the card store. I'll stop by to say hello, assuming I can do that without being mobbed by our fans.

As for your dad, what can I say? He's a super-douche. If

there were a land inhabited just by douches, your dad would be the king. Other douches would bow down to him.

I have to run. Even though I am a rock star, I still have to go work in a men's store in the morning.

Talk to you soon.

Good luck with finals.

And in case you're counting, it's just a few weeks until you get to open your mom's Christmas present! Holy crap! I may have to sneak into your house just so I can see your reaction when you open it!

Scott

Dearest Rock Star,

I loved your tape! We all loved your tape! Me, Dorothy, and Jane, that is. It was so *cool* to finally hear Crush and to hear you sing! And not just because Dorothy had to give *Thriller* a break for a few hours! We had to listen to the tape several times because we were all talking over each other the first few times. Dorothy kept saying, "Is that Scott? Is that Scott's guitar? Is that Scott singing?" Jane made me pull out one of your old letters so she could sing along with the lyrics to "You Don't Know Me." (I told you she's a drama geek, right?) I was thrilled to hear you guys, but also a little emotional about the lyrics and how much they mean to you. Did you sing "Daddy Issues" or "Facial Tissues," or whatever you're calling it these days? It wasn't on the tape, and we'd all really like to hear that one, too.

And what about that song "Have a Heart"? Is that one of your songs, or is it a cover? If it's a cover, whose song is it? And if it's yours, I LOVE it.

I'm so excited for you, Scott, and obviously you're excited, too. Am I even going to recognize you when I get home next week? Should I be expecting spiked hair, tattoos, and multiple piercings? I mean, warn me now, because I have enough change waiting for me at home over Christmas. The last thing I need is for Billy Idol to come walking across the street to knock on the front door. (Ha, you didn't think I'd know who Billy Idol is, did you?)

By the way, Dorothy has been asking to visit "me" over

Christmas break. Since you've specifically said that she's *not* your girlfriend, I've been evasive and told her that I need to make sure that my mom is up for having houseguests. Actually, I know for a fact that my mom wants me to have as many friends as possible around over the holidays, and she's told me multiple times to invite Dorothy and Jane and anyone else I want to stay with us. But this thing between you and Dorothy is more your business than mine, so it would be helpful if you could write to me one more time (or call and actually speak to *me*) and let me know if you want to see Dorothy over Christmas break, okay? We've got almost three full weeks of vacation, so if you want to see her, we'll have time once I get home to plan the details and make sure we get to go to one of your gigs. I'd just like to know how to leave it with her before we leave campus. (And how cool is it that we're talking about your "gigs," by the way?)

You might get the chance to meet James, too. He lives about an hour away from us, between Baltimore and Greenbelt, and we've talked about going for a run down around the Inner Harbor over break. I'm not sure if he's my "boyfriend" since all we do is run together, but he's a nice guy, and there really isn't an opportunity to actually date someone during finals. We met in the art reading room at the Z. All the undergrads have a "reading period," which is a week between the end of classes and the start of exams to do nothing but study. On the first night of reading period, I'd fallen asleep on my notebook when a bloodcurdling scream erupted from about 150 people on the quad in front of the library. In some weird throwback to the '60s and '70s, the students release exam stress by participating in a group "Primal Scream" at midnight each night. That's a terrifying way to wake up, let me tell you. According to James, I sat bolt upright in my chair, screamed, and threw my highlighter in the air. When I was able to focus, there he was, standing in front of me, holding out my highlighter. He smiled and said, "Why don't you let me walk you back to your dorm?" I wiped the drool off my chin, and the fairy tale began. (I'm kidding about it being a fairy tale!)

Seriously, though, he lives in the boys' dorm closest to mine. I'd seen him around, but I hadn't talked to him before. On the way back to my dorm, he told me that he sees me running and asked if I'd like to run with him. I usually run by myself, but to be honest, the Public Safety Department and our resident advisors have been making me really nervous with all their warnings about not running around campus alone, so I accepted his invitation. Since then, we've run together almost every day. He's very different from Walter. Instead of saying that I have a nice ass, James says that I have a beautiful stride. And even though he only sees me without makeup, sweaty, and red-faced, he still shows up at exactly 4:00 p.m. every day to stretch and go running.

That's pretty much been my life for the past two weeks. While you've been becoming a Rock Star, I've been studying, writing a paper, running with James, listening to Crush, and actually taking some exams.

And I'm ready to be done with exams, but I can't say that I'm ready to come home. I had to write a paper about "Duality in Frankenstein," which can be summed up as "People have both good and evil in them." Throw in a few quotes, rework that phrase about twenty times, and—*voila!*—you've got a five-page paper. It took me way too long to write it, though (I totally blew my PINK English periods on the schedule), because I couldn't stop thinking about the "Duality in My Dad." I've tried so hard to get through exams by not thinking about him and his pregnant hosebag, but having to write that paper made it impossible. I ended up wasting hours thinking about stuff like, How could he sit smiling at the family dinner table knowing that he's having an affair with his secretary? How could he kiss me on the forehead every night after he'd slept with her? Why did he invite me to join them for dinner on Christmas Eve? I know you keep calling him a super-douche, but the truth is, he wasn't always like this. He used to be a really good dad.

I'm trying not to think about it because I still have to take my Biology exam, but the closer I get to Christmas break, the harder it is not to think about it. I even participated in the "Primal Scream" earlier tonight, and guess what? It was *awesome.* Okay, so maybe not *quite* as awesome as hearing a bar full of people sing along to your song, but still, kind of awesome. I'd scream again right now if I could, but Dorothy is asleep over there and she would totally throttle me. Has she told you about her new workout routine? She's getting really strong. She and Jane and some of the other girls on the hall spend their BLUE periods doing Jane Fonda workout tapes. I run with James, they "Do Jane" (their phrase, not mine), we all eat dinner together when the Pit opens at 5:30, and then we scatter to our favorite studying spots. How can being a Rock Star beat that?

All right, it's really late, and Dorothy's snoring is totally lulling me to sleep. I'll see you soon. Let me know what to say to Dorothy. I'll try to sneak a word in when she's not making up lyrics to the new Michael Jackson album.

Love,
Cath

P.S. Good luck at your next gig!

P.P.S. Can you send us some of your Crush logo stickers? We'll put them on our door and our backpacks, and before you know it, everyone will insist that you play at one of the events on campus.

December 14, 1982

Cath—

Here's a tape from the show we did last night at the bowling alley. They did this thing called "Rock 'N' Bowl Night" where they had us playing in the bar while people were still bowling. So if you hear any bowling pins getting knocked over in the background, that's why.

And if the suspense is killing you, I can end it for you before you even pop the tape in: yes, we TOTALLY ROCKED AGAIN!

Scott

December 15, 1982

Cath—

Okay, our letters keep crossing in the mail. I just sent you a tape of our show from the bowling alley. Hopefully, you had a chance to listen to it already. We TOTALLY ROCKED, as I'm sure you'll agree. Everyone seems to like to sing along to the chorus of "You Don't Know Me." And we played "Facial Tissues" live for the first time, which is near the end of the tape (as you already know if you've had a chance to listen to it).

"Have a Heart" is one of our own songs. I thought I sent you the lyrics before, didn't I? Anyway, I kind of co-wrote it with Joe. I did the lyrics, and he worked with me on the music, particularly the guitar riff midway through the song (which I think he stole from the Stones, but who cares?) I have to admit that I'm pretty proud of the chorus: "If this thing between us is gonna start / The first thing is, you'd better have a heart."

I'm enclosing about a dozen Crush stickers for you and Jane. I am sending some to Dorothy separately. She mentioned to me that she might be coming to visit "you" over the Christmas break, which is completely cool with me. It would be great if you and she could come see us play at Duffy's one Thursday night, but I do have to warn you that I'm not going to be able to take much time off work over the holidays, so you're going to

143

have to babysit her while she's here. If that's okay with you, great.

Todd's actually working out pretty well at the store. I wouldn't be surprised if my dad wanted to hire him to work on weekends after the holiday season, although that might not happen if Todd doesn't get a haircut soon. To quote my dad, "His hair's longer than Lynda Carter's." (She's the one who played Wonder Woman on TV. My dad has a crush on her.) Hopefully, it won't be too awkward for you to see him. After the debacle with Samantha during the Thanksgiving party, I hope you'll go out of your way to be nice to Todd and introduce him to your new boyfriend James. (Yes, James is your "boyfriend." And, yes, saying you have a "beautiful stride" means he thinks you have a nice ass. It's just like telling a girl you like her sweater or her blouse. That means you like her chest. In case you were wondering.)

I saw your mom at the card shop during my lunch break the other day. (That's not supposed to be related to the last sentence.) She seems to be enjoying it so far, although I doubt she'd tell me if she weren't. And she asked me what I thought of the Christmas gift she got you. I told her you're going to LOVE it! (It's killing me, keeping this to myself! This is the greatest thing in the history of mankind! "Better than the moon landing?" you ask. Yes!)

I haven't had a super-douche sighting since he stole your mom's TV set on Thanksgiving. I understand what you mean when you say that he wasn't always a super-douche. But Superman wasn't always Superman either, was he?

I just realized that I never mention *my* mom in my letters. That's odd, isn't it? Well, she's doing great. She's still helping out at the church a few days a week, and she still reads books like no one's business. She joined the Book of the Month Club—twice. I'm not kidding. It's the only way she can keep getting enough books. She has one membership under the name Cecilia Agee (which you know is her real name) and one under the name Betsy Agee (which is what she calls her *car*). How funny is that—her car has a membership in a book club. Anyway, she's looking forward to seeing you when you come home. My mom, not her car. She's very proud of you and your various achievements. And she's so proud of the role she played in helping your mom pick out your Christmas present. ("Better than the day that guy invented the telephone?" Yes!) And she's also looking forward to meeting Dorothy. Or, as my mom calls her, "the Girl from Catherine's College Who Used to Call and Hang Up."

Hope your Biology exam goes well. (See, I read the boring part of your letter.) And thanks for making me look up the word "duality." I actually had to go all the way downstairs, walk down to the den, get the dictionary off the shelf, look the word up, then put the dictionary back on the shelf, walk back upstairs, and go back to my bedroom. I only mention that so you'll be more careful about using words I don't know in the future. I shouldn't have to exert myself to read a letter.

Okay, I'm going to sign off for now. Lots of clothes to sell to boys and men in the morning.

Scott

P.S. Quote of the day. Some guy was hanging around talking about John F. Kennedy with my dad, and he asked my dad, "Where were you when Kennedy was killed?" And my dad said, "Oh, no, I don't have an alibi!" It was actually pretty funny, but maybe you had to be there.

P.P.S. Don't tell Dorothy, but two different girls gave me their phone numbers after the "Rock 'N' Bowl" gig. I haven't called either one and probably won't, but let me tell you, they both have beautiful strides. I mean, seriously incredible strides.

P.P.P.S. "Better than when Noah built his ark?" Yes! "Better than when *The Brady Bunch* went to Hawaii?" Yes! "Better than going downstairs to look up the word 'duality'?" Yes, yes, yes!

December 18, 1982

Dear Scott,

Just a couple of quick things. I have my last final Tuesday afternoon, but then I have to hang around for another day because I couldn't get a ride home until Wednesday. I'm so exhausted! I just want to get home and sleep in my own bed, with Plum cuddled up next to me.

Okay, here are the quick things:

1. "Facial Tissues" is great. We all loved it. But please change it back to "Daddy Issues." I'm completely fine with that, and the lyrics are much better than "Facial Tissues." (Although "Blow your nose / I've got facial tissues" might be the greatest non sequitur in the history of rock music.)

2. Dorothy was mildly excited to be invited to visit "me." And by "mildly excited" I mean she hasn't stopped grinning like the Cheshire Cat since I extended the invitation.

3. I'm glad that things are working out for Todd at the store. Does he still smell like gasoline? Joking! Don't get all sensitive on me, now. And thanks for the etiquette tip on how to treat him. I'll pull out my manners handbook and reread the "Do the Opposite of What Samantha Drew Would Do" chapter just to make sure that I behave properly. Have a little faith, Rock Star. Geez, Louise.

4. If Dorothy is not your *girlfriend,* then James is definitely not my *boyfriend.* When he said, "You have a beautiful stride," I really think that's what he meant. He's never even tried to kiss me. He may

not even like girls, if you know what I mean. And he's almost too nice. He's nice to the point of being boring. But maybe that's the final exams talking. Who knows? I just want to get out of here for a while. You can judge for yourself if he comes to visit. Maybe he'll give you his phone number and the mystery of whether he's my boyfriend—or yours—will be solved.

See you Saturday!

Love,
Cath

P.S. Enough already about my Christmas present. It can't be any worse than what my parents got me for my last birthday.

P.P.S. Sorry to make you have to look up the word "duality." It sounded brutal. You had to go all the way *downstairs*? To look at a *dictionary*? Poor baby.

Wishing You a Merry Christmas and
a Happy New Year!

Scott,

It's Christmas Eve. I know you're working all day, but I wanted to drop off your present so you'll have it in the morning. I hope you don't hate it. It will make me proud to see you sporting my college colors. (Oops, I just spoiled the surprise. At least I didn't mention that it's a T-shirt. Oops, I did it again! At least I didn't tell you there's no Santa! Oh no, I did it again!)

You guys were great at Duffy's last night. You TOTALLY ROCKED!

Please come over after you and your family have opened your presents. My house is still across the street. It's the one without the TV!

Merry Christmas!

Love,
Cath

P.S. Sorry for the weird kiss. I was just happy for you. And a little drunk. But mostly happy.

December 24, 1982

Cath—

Wait, we're exchanging Christmas presents? When have we *ever* exchanged Christmas presents? (The answer is never. We have *never* exchanged Christmas presents.)

It's too late to go out and get you something, so I hope you'll enjoy finding a nicely wrapped, slightly used box of Wheaties on your front step on Christmas morning. (Oops, I ruined the surprise! At least I didn't mention that they're stale. Oops, I did it again!)

Thanks for coming to the show last night. Sorry we didn't get a chance to talk afterwards, but, you know, the fans come first. And trust me, yours wasn't the weirdest kiss I got that night. Remind me to tell you about the waitress with the red hair.

I'll be listening for your scream when you open your mom's Christmas present in the morning! I've got my window open so I won't miss it.

Merry Christmas!

Scott

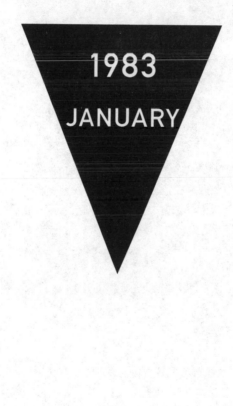

1983
JANUARY

January 4, 1983

Dear Cath—

I know you're visiting Jane for a few days and that you won't get this until you return to school, but we really should talk soon about what happened when you were home for Christmas.

We really should talk about what happened with you and James.

And what happened with me and James.

And what happened with me and Dorothy.

And what happened with you and Dorothy.

And what happened with Dorothy and James.

And what happened with you and your mom.

And what happened with you and your dad's secretary.

And what happened with your mom and your dad's secretary.

And what happened with you and your dad.

And what happened with your mom and your dad.

And what happened with your dad and my dad.

And what happened with you and Todd.

And what happened with me and Todd.

And what happened with my dad and Todd.

And if there's some combination of people I missed, please forgive me. I just feel like if we don't talk soon, we're not going to talk for a very long time. Do you know what I mean? There's a lot to talk about. Everything is just too weird right now.

155

I hope you enjoy the rest of your Christmas break. Give me a call when you get this letter. You know the number.

Scott

P.S. Thanks again for the T-shirt. I'm enclosing one of the Crush T-shirts we made. Now that the band has broken up, there's no reason for anyone to buy one anymore.

P.P.S. My mom insisted that I include a note from her with my letter, so I am doing it.

January 4, 1983

Dearest Catherine,

It was so wonderful to see you when you were in town and to meet your lovely roommate! And it's so nice that you and Scottie have kept in touch. He gets very excited when he sees he got a letter from you! Thank you for taking the time out of your busy academic schedule for him.

I am so glad to hear that you loved your mother's Christmas present. I was with her when she first saw it at the mall, and we were both so excited when we stumbled across it. I know things have been difficult for you with everything going on at home, and I was literally just saying to your mother that you need to "just hang in there" when we saw the beautiful, framed picture of the cat hanging from the tree limb with the words HANG IN THERE, BABY! written on it. They are truly inspirational words perfect for a truly inspirational girl!

I am sorry about what happened between Mr. Agee and your father, but I'm going to stay out of that. We can let the men work things out for themselves.

Have a great semester at school. We are all so proud of you.

Love,
Mrs. Agee

January 4, 1983

Scott,

I saw this postcard and thought of you.
I'm waiting for Jane to pick me up at the train station outside her hometown.
That was a nightmare. That was *not* the way I wanted to end Christmas break.
I hope you and I are okay. I'll call you as soon as I get back to Wake.

Cath

158

Dear Scott,

Jane and I just got back to school. It was so nice to have a few days
with her and her family after all the craziness at home. During the
entire time I was at her house, there wasn't a single fistfight, no one
yelled at anyone, and there wasn't a single moment when I felt like
banging my head against the fucking wall. Can you imagine that?
Anyway, we came back early because Jane is going to rush a sorority. She's trying to talk me into it, but I'm not sure it's for me. We'll
see. In the meantime, I have a whole quiet Sunday in front of me to
write to you.

I got your letter as soon as I got back to school and tried to call
you right away. What do you mean Crush broke up? Why would you
do that? You guys were great and everything seemed to be going so
well. I hope it didn't have anything to do with that last night at
Duffy's. Or more precisely, all the stuff that happened *after* that last
night at Duffy's. What a mess! I've called you a few times, but I keep
getting your mom on the phone. I love talking to her, but, seriously,
I can only fake my way through the whole "Thank you for helping
my mom pick out that poster for me—it's perfect!" thing so many
times. And, honestly, it's a little uncomfortable given what happened
between our dads, so I may have to pull a Dorothy and start hanging up if your mom answers the phone.

When are you ever home, anyway? I thought I'd see you a lot
more over break. Between your shifts at the store, your rehearsals,

my catching up with the girls, and then Dorothy wanting you all to herself, I feel like we hardly even saw each other. Your hair looks good long, by the way.

You asked a lot of questions in your letter. I can't answer them all, but I'll take a swing at a few of them.

I'll start with you and me and James and Dorothy. In no particular order. Well, I guess the bottom line is that I owe everybody a big, fat apology for walking away from Duffy's that night. I'm really sorry that you and Dorothy had to deal with James and convince him to go home. I can't totally explain what happened. James seemed like such a nice, smart, polite guy during exams. And you saw him. He's a little on the skinny side, but he's a tall, good-looking guy. I assumed that something would develop between us—which is why I joked that he might be "College Boyfriend #2." When he came to visit and we couldn't go running because of the snow, we hung around the house all day and I realized that I just don't like him *that* way, if you know what I mean. He *is* a nice, smart, polite guy. But he is also somehow *too* nice, to the point of being oddly protective and concerned about me. He almost cried when I told him how weird it felt being home alone and how my mom and I used to bake nonstop over the holidays for all the people in my dad's office. I mean, yeah, it's sad, but I don't need a boy hanging around who's going to get all weepy on me. Jesus.

At Duffy's that night, after he had a few beers, James kept gazing at me like a sad sack and then he started touching me and massaging my shoulders in a really uncomfortable way. I don't know if you could see that from the stage, but it was just weird. I needed to get away from him and the whole scene. I only meant to go outside to get some air. But then Todd came out and we just started walking.

I'm sorry that I left without saying anything to anyone. I know that was uncool and that everyone had to hang around and wonder if you should wait for me to come back or try to find me or whatever. Thanks for your note telling me that you're not mad. I've been worried about that. Dorothy and I didn't talk much when she drove me to the train station on her way home the next day. She claimed to be hungover. I don't know what else you're referring to in your letter about "what happened with me and Dorothy." She's not back here yet, so I don't have a clue.

Now to try to address what happened with my mom and dad and Todd and the secretary, in no particular order—

So you already know that Christmas Eve was hard for me. Seeing my dad and his slutty secretary playing house and having to deal with her relatives left me with an enormous headache and huge knots in my stomach. I still can't stop thinking about his hat perched on the shelf of the coat closet. Or the way the secretary kept referring to me as "her." Or the way he kept touching her belly.

I "forgot" to take their present with me when I left after Christmas Eve dinner. Truthfully, I had no interest in receiving a gift from them, but I guess my dad really wanted me to have it before I came back to school. He and the secretary drove to our house that last night when we were all at Duffy's. My mother was *furious* that he would bring "That Woman" to our house. You've probably gotten the whole story from your parents, but I guess my parents started yelling at each other and attracted the attention of some of the neighbors. Todd and I drove up in the middle of everything, and my dad was furious with me for being "out after curfew," which was ridiculous since I'm in college and my mom agreed that I don't have a curfew. Anyway, this is how I remember it: Your dad came across the street, saying something like, "Now, Jim, why don't you just settle down. Catherine's home safe and sound and everything's fine." I'm embarrassed to repeat this, Scott, I really am, but my dad wheeled around and said, "What the hell would you know about paying college tuition for your kid to hang out with a grease monkey until all hours of the night?" and then, boom, my dad was laid out on the sidewalk. I'm pretty sure your dad punched him in the face. It all happened so fast that I can't swear to it. Maybe my dad slipped on the ice, maybe your dad pushed him, I really don't know. It was *very* uncool, though.

You and I have joked about your dad beating up my dad, but when that happened, it was terrible. My mom and I screamed and rushed to help my dad, and the secretary jumped out of the car and yelled, "You get away from him!" I don't know if she was talking to me, or my mom, or both of us. Anyway, my mom and I both took a step back, the secretary helped my dad get up, and they hobbled to their big shiny car and drove away.

We were all stunned. No one could speak. Everyone sort of drifted back into their houses, and I walked Todd to his truck, where he summed it all up by saying, "I see what you mean about everything being different."

My mom and I were restless and decided to take down the Christmas tree. We usually have fun with it and listen to Christmas music for one last time, but not this year. We worked like silent robots until every last light and ornament was wrapped, stacked, and back in the attic. Then we went to bed and didn't even wake up when Dorothy came in.

The next morning, before Dorothy and I left for the train station, my mom said, "I hope your father doesn't sue Mr. Agee. He was only trying to help." And I know he was trying to help. I know he was, Scott, but, man, that was a mess. As much as my dad has hurt my mom and me lately, that night made me realize that he's the only dad I'll ever have. Super-douche or no super-douche, I don't want to see him hurt like that again.

And something else that totally surprised me—I was scared for the baby when the Slutty Secretary jumped out of the car and came running up the slippery sidewalk. I almost yelled, "Slow down, stupid!" before she told me, or my mom, or both of us not to touch my dad.

As far as what happened between me and Todd, nothing happened between me and Todd. We walked, I talked, he listened. He put his arm around me when I got cold. There was a beautiful half moon glistening off the snow and for maybe an hour, my head cleared, my stomach didn't hurt, and it felt like 1983 might not be so bad after all. Of course, that feeling didn't last too long.

The real question is, what the hell happened between *you* and Todd? Why did the band break up? I've never seen you as happy as you were playing with Crush. Please call or write soon. Or maybe just write since, if you call, Dorothy will hog the phone anyway.

Holy cow. It's 4 p.m. and guess who just showed up with his running gear? Seriously, James, take a hint. I do need a run, though.

Write soon, okay?

Love,
Cath

January 11, 1983

Cath—

Look, I wasn't there, but my mom says that your dad pushed my dad first. Maybe you didn't see it, or maybe you don't remember it because you were drunk, but that's what she says. My dad was trying to keep your super-douche of a dad from making any more of a scene than he already was because you were out late with Todd, and your super-douche of a dad pushed my dad and told him to mind his own business. That's when my dad pushed him back. He didn't *punch* your dad—he *pushed* him. That's what my mom says, and I believe her. If your dad is such a wimp that he falls down when he gets pushed, that's his problem, not my dad's. And if your dad says my dad punched him, then he's a liar. But we already know he's a liar, don't we?

And I'm sorry, but if you think the fight was uncool, then your dad threatening to call the police was *really* uncool.

I'm sorry if that's a bit rougher than what you expected to hear, but I'm not going to sit back and listen to people talk trash about my dad. Not only did my dad have to deal with that crap with your dad, but he also had to deal with crap with your old boyfriend Todd. My dad gave Todd a decent job at the store and was going to hire him full-time to keep working there. And what did Todd do? He was giving his employee discount to practically everyone who came into the store. It probably cost my dad about a thousand bucks. All Todd had to do was apologize and everything probably would have been fine with him and my dad. And I told Todd that if he didn't apologize to my dad, the band was finished. But he wouldn't apologize. He kept saying, "Tell your fat, stupid father that an employee discount is an employee's to use however he wants, and I'm not going to apologize if I want to use it with a lot of people." So my dad—who may be fat, but isn't stupid—fired him. And now the band is finished, too. At least until we find a new drummer to replace Todd, which shouldn't be that hard. Replacing his van might be more difficult.

By the way, if you don't know what happened with you and Dorothy, maybe you should ask her. I know you don't like her, Cath, but I do, and I can certainly see why she would feel that you ignored her or that you were acting as if you were embarrassed to be seen with her while you were home.

Scott

P.S. I know you and I both think your mom's Christmas gift was pretty ridiculous, but here's an idea. Why don't you have your mom send it to you, and you can give it to Dorothy, who would love it. (No comment.) That way you don't have to keep it, and you end up making both of them happy.

P.P.S. Do you have a van?

January 19, 1983

Dear Scott,

I let some time go by before replying to your letter because I was hoping you'd think twice about some of the things you said and send me another letter, but I guess that's not going to happen. I've started many different versions of a reply to you over the past few days.

There was the "I can't believe we've been friends all our lives and you'd send me such a stupid letter" reply, which initially, I really liked. It went through a few iterations. (Go look up "iterations" in the dictionary if you need to. It's all the way downstairs in the den. Sorry, that was mean.) There was the short version, along the lines of "Nice to know you've regressed to being a twelve-year-old boy." And there was a longer version, like "No, I don't really like Dorothy, but I invited her to my house over the first profoundly awkward and confusing holiday since my parents split up only to make *you* happy, you big dope, so maybe you should be somewhat grateful rather than thick as a brick."

I decided not to send that letter. You're welcome.

There was also the totally pissed-off reply that included something about how I have no control over how Todd uses his goddamn employee discount, and a suggestion about sticking the framed cat poster up your Rocker Dude ass. Which actually would be rather difficult since I carried it all the way back here on the bus. Why would you think that I would leave my mother's gift to me at home?

167

And there's no room to stick a poster up your ass anyway since your head is already wedged up there.

But I decided not to send that letter, either. You're welcome.

The weird thing is, though, that each letter, no matter how it started, ended up being an "I really hate it when we don't get along" letter. Because I do. I fucking hate it. This never used to happen when we lived across the street from each other. Or if we did have a problem, it always got fixed within a few hours, and we'd end up on the couch watching TV and eating cookies.

Look, I know that everything was a shitmess over Christmas break. I couldn't be more sorry that your family got pulled into my family's craziness. I think I already told you that I don't really know exactly what happened between our dads or how my dad ended up on the ground. I'm sorry if people are saying bad things. I would never say anything bad about your dad to anyone. I'm almost afraid to tell you this, but my dad is driving down here to take me to lunch next week. I'm very nervous about it. I don't know if he wants me to testify or whatever about that night, but don't worry. I'll tell him that it all happened so fast, I didn't really see anything clearly.

So please, Scott, with everything else that's going on, let's not fight, okay? I mean, yeah, the Dorothy visit was a bit of a debacle. But cut me some slack here. You have to admit that you fooling around with my college roommate is a bit weird. Maybe we should reestablish the Samantha Guidelines—you don't talk to me about Dorothy or to Dorothy about me, and I'll stay out of it entirely, unless someone's sanity or life is in danger. (And yes, I still maintain that it was reasonable to assume that someone's life was in danger given the noises that were coming from the backseat of your car after Homecoming last year, so let's not discuss *that* again.)

It might be a little more complicated because I live with Dorothy, but, really, we don't see each other much anyway. She's going through sorority rush, and I'm working a bunch of shifts at the Pizza Pan, running with get-a-clue James, and trying to stay current on my new classes. And it's not like you're going to get married, right? RIGHT?!?!

What are you doing about Crush? I was talking to Billy, my manager at work, about how great you guys are. He listened to your tapes, and he really wants you to play in the Battle of the Bands. He runs it every year on the night that all the sorority wannabes sit in their dorms waiting for their "bids." The boys on campus have nothing to do but come to the Pizza Pan to drink beer and listen to good music. I'll be working behind the bar that night. You should come down, if you've figured out your drummer situation. (And you know I don't have a van. Can't you fit all your equipment in Betsy?)

So, are we okay? Because if I haven't mentioned it before, I really hate it when we don't get along. Should we talk on the phone? Do I need to come up there and sit under a clothes rack and hold my breath until we're okay again? Is this worse than when I made you laugh when you were serving on the altar and Father Martin made you sweep the entire parking lot after Mass? Worse than when I left you at the gas station because you wouldn't stop singing "California Dreamin'" after I met that boy at summer camp? Worse than when

169

I gave you a stale box of cereal for Christmas? Oh wait. That was you. And somehow it still wasn't the worst Christmas present I got.

Write me. Or call. You know the number.

Your friend (yes?),

Cath

P.S. Even if I don't hear from you, I'll write to tell you about the lunch with my dad next week.

P.P.S. Have you seen *Tootsie* yet? I went to see it with Jane and her family. It's about an actor (Dustin Hoffman) who dresses up as a woman to get a part on a soap opera, and he ends up learning a lot about himself. The reason I mention it is that, when we went out for hot chocolate afterwards, Jane's father said he liked how the movie dealt with the duality of mankind. I swear I choked on my hot chocolate when he said "duality."

P.P.P.S. Here's something that I know will get a smile out of you. Walter broke his leg skiing over Christmas break. He's hobbling around campus on his crutches looking pathetic. That's called karma, dude.

WORLD OF FLOWERS

1/22/83

Dear Cath—

Sorry I was such a dudebag.

Are we still Tomatoes?

Scott

January 24, 1983

Dear Cath—

"Dudebag"? It was supposed to say "douchebag." I don't even know what a "dudebag" is. But I'm glad it got a laugh out of you, and I'm glad we got a chance to talk last night, even if it was only for a few minutes.

Anyway, I really am sorry for being such a dudebag. You know how they tell you that you shouldn't drive when you're drunk? Well, apparently I shouldn't write letters when I'm angry. And I wasn't angry with you. I was angry with the whole ridiculous situation. Or ridiculous situations, plural. And I guess I ended up taking it out on you because I couldn't take it out on the people I'm really ticked off at. So please forgive me. If you haven't already thrown my last letter in the trash, please do it as soon as you can. And tear it up into little pieces first. I don't need Dorothy pulling it out of the trash and figuring out what a dudebag I can be. Although, between me and you, I have a feeling she sometimes reads the letters I write to you while you're out of the room. There are things she knows that she couldn't know otherwise, unless you told her. Like there's no way she'd know the chorus of "Have a Heart." (If you're reading this one, Dorothy, hello! How are you? Are you aware that reading someone else's mail is a federal offense? Or it may be. I'm not a lawyer.)

Anyway, Dorothy gave me a full report on her first semester grades. I'm assuming you've already heard all about them

172

and have tried to be as supportive as I have tried to be, whether you like her or not. I'm sure a lot of people who are used to getting straight A's in high school don't get straight A's when they get to college, where everyone is just as smart and you don't have people like me pitching in at the bottom of the grading curve. (You're welcome, by the way.) Hopefully, she's not too depressed and will do better this semester.

But that made me realize something—I haven't heard a word from you about *your* grades for the first semester. Nothing. Not a sound. That could mean you got great grades and don't want to brag. Or it could mean that you got Dorothy-esque grades and are too embarrassed to talk about it. Or it could just mean that you don't want to tell me because I'm a dudebag. Anyway, I'm curious. If you want to tell me, I'm all ears.

In case you were wondering, we are still without a drummer. I see our former drummer, who shall remain nameless, driving around town in his van all the time. And I have to admit that I get a little misty-eyed when that happens because, deep down, I really, really do miss . . . his van. It was perfect for hauling all our equipment, as well as a case of beer. Without it, we're stuck. I wish all our equipment would fit into Betsy, but it's not even close. Anyhow, we auditioned a couple of drummers last week, and they completely and totally sucked balls. One was a senior over at Glendale High who talked a great game, but couldn't keep a beat to save his life. He played the drums like a guy being attacked by a swarm of bees, if you can picture that.

The other one was a guy who used to play drums in that band the Runaway Devils that you and I saw when we went down to Fells Point a couple years back. Only it wasn't the drummer who played with them when we saw them, and we quickly learned why he said he "used to play" with them, as opposed to "is currently playing" with them—he is madly in love with his cymbals. Every song, it's cymbals, cymbals, cymbals. *Ping, ping, ping, ping, ping.* It makes you want to pull your hair out. From the inside. We won't be using either one of them. Even though the cymbal guy did have a van. A beautiful van. The type of van a guy could fall in love with. The type of van that has a beautiful stride.

By the way, I'm writing a new song called "Um." I'll send you the lyrics when I'm done with it. It's a little rowdier than the other songs I've written, a little punkier. Kind of like the Undertones, if you know who they are. And there isn't a single cymbal in the entire song. It is completely, entirely, 100% *ping*-free.

Let's talk soon.

Again, my apologies for being a dudebag. You know I care about you a ton, right?

Scott

P.S. I feel like I used "dudebag" one or two times too many in this letter. Your thoughts?

P.P.S. Dorothy, if you're reading this letter, when I said "I care about you" to Cath, I meant I care about her like a family pet, like a dog or a cat.

P.P.P.S. Cath, I am not saying that you're actually a dog or a cat.

Dear Scott,

I did throw away your last letter, but I will forever keep the "dude-bag" note from the florist. The thought of you saying "Sorry I was such a douchebag" over the phone to some little old florist lady just about kills me every time I think of it. (And, yes, we are still Tomatoes!)

Dorothy is being dramatic about her grades. What a shocker! And why are we talking about her? I thought we had agreed not to talk about her. She maybe got one C sprinkled in amongst her B's. I think she'll live. My grades were fine, under the circumstances. I'm cutting myself some slack. I'm trying to take courses this semester that I'm really interested in, like Art History and Abnormal Psych, because it's easier for me to concentrate when I like the subject matter. Not being able to concentrate was my major issue last semester, and I expect it will be more of the same for a while. I mean, my mom is a little more stable now that we've gotten through the holidays and she is more in the routine of working again, but there's still a lot of drama swirling around the divorce (my dad got a lawyer and had divorce papers served on my mom at the card store) and money and the big fat pregnant secretary waddling around town. Maybe you've seen her?

Speaking of school, though, I'm taking a poetry class with this cool professor named Sally Bishop, and I wanted to ask you if I could share some of your lyrics in class. Don't worry, I'll give you full credit. The Honor Code is a huge deal here, and I don't want to get thrown out of school over "Daddy Issues." Anyway, do you mind? You are a much better writer than the geeks who have volunteered their stuff so far, and I think that song would generate an interesting class discussion.

So here's the latest on my dad and what I have come to think of as "That Night." He drove down here to have lunch with me yesterday. It was a beautiful sunny day, and he took me to a nice resort-type restaurant with a view of Pilot Mountain. We sat looking out at the pine trees, and it reminded me of our family ski vacations. I was really sad and really nervous that he was going to ask me to testify against your dad about the "fight" (or whatever you'd call it). We talked about my grades and school in general, and he was surprisingly mellow about everything. Eventually he brought up the "scene" with your dad That Night, and I braced myself to be tough, but then he just started *crying*. I couldn't believe it. I'd never seen my father cry before. I'd never seen any grown man cry before. He started apologizing for everything. The affair, hurting my mom, hurting me, all his recent "jack-ass behavior." He said that falling on the ice knocked some sense into him. He was very ashamed about having a shouting match in the front yard, and about dragging your dad into it, who he said is someone that he's "known and respected forever." Then he sort of veered off course and rambled about what it's like for a man his age to "have a baby on the way."

I didn't know what to say or do. I mostly just stopped eating and stared hard out the window. I drank his beer, and he either didn't notice or he didn't care. I hope this doesn't sound cruel, but I didn't feel sorry for him at all. I was embarassed that he was crying in a nice restaurant. I wanted him to stop talking and blow his nose. I needed my mother. The whole thing was so far out of my depth. I kept thinking, "I'm just a kid. Isn't there an adult you can talk to about this stuff?"

Anyway, he's not going to sue your dad, so that's good, right? But the rest of it, man, Scott. It should be good, I guess, that he apologized and talked about real stuff, but thinking about it just makes me feel flat and tired. Like, was it all just a waste? He ruined our family and now he's crying about it? I feel like he doesn't have the right to cry about it. He's the one who fucked everything up! I get to cry about it. My mom definitely gets to cry about it. But I don't think he gets to cry about it. Not to me, anyway.

Maybe it was easier when he was being a douchebag and I could be totally pissed off at him. But I don't really know. I don't remember feeling anything but sad for a while now.

I'm sorry this is another one of my bummer letters. I was going to write you a funny letter about watching the girls go through sorority rush, wearing bowler hats with cocktail dresses and blue highheeled shoes, waiting to get their bids this weekend, but obviously I didn't write that letter.

Since you don't have a drummer yet, I assume Crush can't play in the Battle of the Bands. It's too bad. Judging from the band I heard at the Deke House last night, you guys would have no trouble winning. Or maybe not. I was a little drunk and did manage to dance to their cover of Squeeze's "Annie Get Your Gun." (Thanks for introducing me to Squeeze's music last summer!)

Give your mom and dad a hug for me and tell them they don't have to worry about my dad anymore.

And I care about you, too. I won't say I care about you a ton, though, because I'm not sure that's the right unit of measure for those things.

Cath

P.S. I'm looking forward to seeing the lyrics to "Um" because the title doesn't tell me very much about the song. Although it did make me think of you right away because, in case you didn't notice, you do say "um" an awful lot. Not in writing, of course, but in person. I think it's your favorite word!

P.P.S. Why don't you just let Todd back in the band, already? He's a good dude, he doesn't overdo it with the cymbals, and the band makes you so happy. I mean, what are you doing for fun without Crush? Actually, don't tell me. I don't think I want to know.

January 31, 1983

Dear Cath,

So Dorothy told you she got all B's and one C, huh? Well, that's interesting, because she told *me* she got all C's and one D. That's very different, isn't it? So either she's lying to you because she doesn't want you to know how bad her grades really were, or she's lying to me because . . . well, you tell me, you're the Psych student. Why would she do that? Now I need to figure out which one of us she's lying to. I hope it's you because lying about grades to make them sound better is perfectly normal and something I have personal experience with, as do my parents. But lying about your grades to make them sound *worse*? That's just sick.

As for your dad—the other person I thought we weren't going to talk about anymore—I'm glad to hear he's not going to sue my dad and not going to ask you to testify against him. I don't know what to say about your lunch, though. Partly, it's that I'm afraid I'm going to say something to upset you again, and God knows we don't need to be ticking each other off again. But it's also that the whole lunch sounds so strange, you know? I mean, I've never seen my dad cry. He didn't even cry at my grandma's funeral, and he didn't cry that time the lawn mower blade sliced his foot. Fifty stitches, and the guy didn't cry. So if I ever saw him crying at a restaurant in front of however many complete strangers, I don't know what I would do.

Walk out? Call a doctor? Crawl under the table? Tell him to stop being a baby? I just know it would change things.

That wasn't much help, was it? Sorry. I'm not good at this stuff. I'm pretty good at selling clothes, though. Ask me a question about that. I'm at the point now where I can tell what size someone is when they walk through the front door. Jeff Hill's dad was in a couple weeks ago. As soon as he came in, I said to him, "You're a 44 regular, 16-inch neck, 35-inch sleeve." And I was right on the money. Impressive, isn't it? Maybe I should set up a booth at the carnival.

To answer your non-clothes-related question, I haven't seen the pregnant secretary around town at all. Not that I would expect to since I spend very little time hanging around the maternity store. But if I do see her, you'll be the first person to know.

Hold on. Let's go back a second. I just thought of why Dorothy would tell me her grades were worse than they really were—so she could cry on the phone and have me say a lot of sweet things to her. We had some VERY long phone calls where I was telling her not to worry about her grades, and how she'll do better next semester, and how great she is, and how smart she is, and all that stuff boyfriends say to their girlfriends when they're upset. If she lied to me about her grades just so I'd say that stuff to her, that's not cool. Not cool at all. So how do I find out if she lied to me about her grades? Do you think the school would tell me what her grades were if I called up and asked?

What if I pretended to be her father? Do you know what her father's first name is in case I need to do that?

By the way, I'm assuming you're joking about giving one of my songs to your poetry class. I'm not a poet like . . . okay, I thought the name of a poet would come to me, but I can't think of one. Was Shakespeare a poet? If so, I'm not a poet like Shakespeare. I write songs for a band that doesn't exist because we don't have a drummer and we don't have a van. And you can't have a band without a drummer or a van. It's as simple as that. Do you know where the lead singer of Queen would be today without a drummer or a van? He'd be working in his father's clothing store somewhere in England, that's where— "Ye Olde Freddie Mercury Senior's Men's Clothing Shoppe. Where Blokes and Boys Shoppe." They spell things differently in England, you know. God knows why.

Anyway, we auditioned two more drummers last week. One guy had to be 40 years old, and the other guy had long, blond feathered hair like Farrah Fawcett-Majors that he kept flipping with the back of his hand. Seriously creepy. Neither of them could keep a beat to save his life, but at least Farrah has a station wagon that might hold all our equipment if we flip down the backseat. It's not nearly as nice as Todd's van. It's like my mom says—you never know what you have until it's gone, do you? I'll always think of that van as "the one that got away." As for Todd, you might have already heard, but he's back working at the gas station. That means I have to drive to Ridgewood to get gas now because I don't feel like dealing with him and his crap. He'd probably put sugar in my gas tank anyway. And if I saw his van, I might start weeping.

So, we're kind of stuck now. We either have to keep looking for a new drummer with a van, or we add Farrah to the band. We're going to decide tonight.

I haven't finished writing "Um" yet, but I'll send it to you when I do. I haven't really been in a rush to finish it since we can't play it until we get a drummer. The chorus goes like this:

Um, um, um, um,
Um, um, um, um.

I think you'd probably have to hear it.

My mom says hi. I'm sure my dad would say hi, too, but I haven't mentioned you or your family in a while. It's not worth getting him upset. The January, post-holiday sales are getting him upset enough as it is. Hand on Bible, we had one day last week where the only person who came in to the store was the mailman. That's a bad day in the clothing business, as Freddie Mercury's father would tell you.

Have a good week.

Scott

P.S. If I had to grade it, I think this letter would get a B. Although I may be lying about that. It could be an A or a C.

P.P.S. My dad thinks Freddie Mercury is homosexual. Yeah, right. My dad thinks any guy with long hair is homosexual. Wait until he gets a load of Farrah, if he joins the band.

FEBRUARY

Dear Scott,

I'm coming home next weekend—not this one, but the next. I
haven't told Dorothy because I'm afraid she'll want to come with
me if I tell her, and I'd rather come by myself. I know that's really
mean since I'm sure she'd like to see you, but I'd like to get away
from everything related to college for a few days, and that includes
her. You're more than welcome to trade places with me and stay in
our room if you want to visit her, although, as you probably know,
she's trying to get into a sorority right now, so I don't know how
much free time she has anyway. I don't really know what the hell
sororities do, other than wear sweatpants with big Greek letters
sewn on their butts. Which is really hideous, by the way. Particularly when some of the girls don't have a beautiful stride, if you
know what I mean.

Anyway, I just can't handle being here right now. I'm really
tired all the time. The days are so short and dark, and I just need to
come home and sit on the couch with my mom for a few days. With
Jane also going through sorority rush, I've been covering some of
her shifts at the Pizza Pan, and I've also been working some nights
behind the bar, which is better than delivering pizzas in the cold, but
pretty hard work. There's a lot of restocking and some relatively
heavy lifting and, when it's busy, just plain constant motion. Sometimes it's cool to talk to guys when they are relaxed and just sipping

a beer and glancing at a basketball game on the TV, and then sometimes I think I know what you mean about guys you know who come into the store and act like they've never met you before. There are frat boy friends of Walter's who act like they've never met me when they ask for a beer. I go out of my way to use their names as I hand them their drinks and look them in the eye to let them know that I think they're dicks. And some of the girls are masters of denial as well. Due to limited freezer space, the pints of ice cream that you can buy on the meal plan are stored behind the bar. Girls that I delivered a pizza to only two hours before will ask me for a pint of Rocky Road and stand there and tell their friends that they skipped dinner so they could finish a paper or fit into their dress for some rush event. Really? I think the fact that you've been reduced to wearing nothing but sweatpants is a dead giveaway on that fake diet plan. Usually I like my job, though. The other kids I work with are very cool, and I get to drink an unlimited amount of Tab from the fountain dispenser. I still think you should try to schedule a "gig" at the Pizza Pan. My manager still asks me about you guys. People love to see bands there on Friday or Saturday nights, as long as there isn't a basketball game on TV. Baseketball is huge in this state. HUGE, I tell you.

Anyway, I just wanted to let you know about my plans for next weekend. If you don't come to visit Dorothy, maybe we could go out for an early birthday celebration for your 19th while I'm home. Birthday burgers, beer, and bowling?

Much love,

Cath

P.S. Freddie Mercury is gay. Think about it for a second. The name of his band is *Queen*. Mystery solved.

February 3, 1983

Dear Scott:

I guess our letters crossed in the mail. I'm still planning on coming home next weekend, but I don't know if I'll see you, and God knows I can never get the phone to call you at a decent hour, so I'll just write you a quick letter.

Part of your little mystery has been solved. Are you sitting down? Your girlfriend got straight A's last semester, if you include one A-. Should I repeat that? SHE GOT STRAIGHT A's. How do I know? Because her parents sent her a cake that said "Straight-A College Girl" on it in loopy pink icing. She tried to hide it, but come on—our room is the size of a telephone booth. Eventually, she admitted that she got straight A's (including one A-) and said she had told me she got B's and C's because she didn't want to seem like she was bragging, which might make sense if she hadn't spent so much time acting upset about her grades. As for why she told you she got C's and D's, you already seem to have a good working theory on that. My head hurts just thinking about this nonsense.

Please tell me you're not silly enough to drive all the way to Ridgewood to buy gas. Just drop by Todd's gas station and ask him to rejoin the band. Please? He probably doesn't even remember why you threw him out of the band in the first place. Trust me, the guy has no long-term memory. And he's not the type to hold a grudge. I dumped him, and he's still nice to me.

I read "Daddy Issues" aloud in my poetry class and a tall girl in the front row started to cry, so we didn't have such a great discussion about it. Instead, we ended up talking about her parents' divorce. Then we ended up talking about everyone's parents' divorces. Half the class's parents are divorced. I actually felt bad for the kids whose parents are still together. They had nothing to talk about!

My honest reaction to "Um" is *"What-at-at?"* You just sing "um" over and over? Maybe I'm missing something.

You really should be out there singing "Daddy Issues" and "Have a Heart" and your other songs. If I run into Todd next weekend, do you want me to see if he's still pissed off at you?

I hope I'll see you next weekend, but I'll totally understand if you want to visit Dorothy. I'll be home at the end of March for Spring Break anyway. The New Baby is arriving, and all that. Who would want to spend Spring Break partying in Florida when you could be hanging with the Slutty Secretary and a crying infant? So much to look forward to. Hooray for me!

Even if you're not home, I'll stop by to say hi to your mom. I'll steer clear of your dad.

Love,
Cath

February 6, 1983

Cath—

I have to work on Saturday, but I don't think I would have wanted to swap places with you and visit Dorothy this weekend anyway. This whole thing with her grades is so stupid, but I have to admit that it's bugging the hell out of me. At first, I thought that maybe she told me she got C's and D's because she wanted me to feel sorry for her and tell her how great she is, which is exactly what I did. Then I started to think that maybe she told me she got C's and D's because she thinks I'm a moron who isn't even going to college, and she thought I'd feel uncomfortable dating a smart girl. Anyway, I ended up talking with my dad about it at work today while we were waiting for anyone to come in, and his response was today's Quote of the Day: "Maybe you're just dating a nutbar." Then, for the rest of the day, he kept calling her "Snickers." Because Snickers bars have nuts in them, in case that wasn't clear. Maybe he's right. Maybe she's just plain nuts.

Also, I am NOT going to beg Todd to rejoin the band, and I am more than happy to drive to Ridgewood for gas just to avoid dealing with him. While I understand that he still talks to you even after you dumped him, you had a very different relationship with Todd than I did. Very different. Very, VERY different. I could draw pictures if you'd like. Anyway, he can kiss my ass. We are more than happy to have Farrah playing the drums for us—and our stuff fits in his station wagon after all. It looks like we may have a couple gigs later in the month, and we're actually going to be rehearsing in our garage on Sunday when you're home visiting. Maybe you can stop by and listen to us. I really think you need to hear "Um" to appreciate it. Plus, you can meet Farrah and his incredible, lifelike hair.

By the way, the secretary is finally going to give birth? Is it just me, or does it seem like she's been pregnant for a couple years now? Isn't there a nine-month statute of limitations on those things? Is it possible she's faking it and just has a couple pillows shoved up her sweater?

See you this weekend. Burgers, beer, and bowling sounds great. You can call me at the store to set up the time. Just don't call when we're busy, which is . . . never. And if my dad answers, just hang up. He'll assume it was Todd calling.

Scott

P.S. Please don't call Farrah "Farrah" when you meet him. His real name is Robert. He doesn't know we call him "Farrah."

P.P.S. Please don't tell Dorothy that my dad calls her "Snickers," either.

P.P.P.S. Hey, Dorothy, if you happen to be reading Cath's mail again while she's out of the room, guess what—my dad calls you "Snickers"! Because Snickers have nuts, in case that wasn't clear.

February 9, 1983

Dear Scott,

I don't know what to say about Dorothy and why she would lie to you about her grades. But I have to tell you that if she tells you that she didn't get into any of the sororities that she wanted, she won't be lying. She's not just trying to get your sympathy. She's the only girl on our hall who went through rush and didn't get a bid from the one she wanted. It was really awful to see the other girls jumping up and down and hugging each other while she ducked into our room to cry. I totally don't get it. She really wants to do all that girly-girl groupy stuff and would be so into wearing the letters and all that jazz—why won't they let her in?

Jane got into her first choice and was very sweet to Dorothy about how stupid and random the process is, but Dorothy was crying too much to hear most of what Jane had to say. Dorothy's parents are so worried about her that they are flying her home for the weekend. Selfishly, I'm glad of that so you don't have to deal with her legitimate blubbering while still wondering about the fake grades thing, and I would've felt awful about not inviting her to come home with me. I do feel sorry for her, but I also really need a few good nights' sleep. I've become a total insomniac here lately and end up most nights sleeping from around midnight to 2 a.m., when I wake up with my mind racing and no hope of falling back asleep. I usually migrate to the commons room to do some reading or writing, and I've found that 5 a.m. is a really peaceful time to fall asleep on the couch down there. I still usually have time to run and shower before my first class, so it's not terrible, but when you see me, you'll probably notice that I could use a good night's sleep.

As for the Slutty Secretary, I try not to obsess about the details, but if you count back 9 months from her March due date, I'm guessing she got pregnant sometime last summer. Our Spring Break is the last week of March, and my dad has made it very clear that he expects me to be home to meet my "little brother or sister." This whole thing is so weird. It just doesn't feel like how my life is supposed to be happening. And I really don't feel like having a little brother or sister right now. I'd rather have a beer.

Anyway, I'm looking forward to one of our classic bowling evenings together. I'll call you at the store when I get home. I promise not to talk about myself the whole time if you promise not to yell "There it is!" every time you get a strike. It's obnoxious, and not in a way that grows on you over time. Trust me.

Love,
Cath

P.S. Happy Valentine's Day! Or Happy Pal-entine's Day, in our case!

CEDAR CREEK
HOSPITAL

February 10, 1983

Dear Cath,

I'm assuming we'll talk or I'll see you before you get this, but I feel like writing this down anyway. I tried to reach you half a dozen times tonight, but Dorothy said you were out for the night. Hopefully, we'll talk before you head up here for the weekend.

By the time you see this, you'll understand why this is being written on Cedar Creek Hospital stationery. For all the times we have joked about how my dad was going to have a heart attack because of his weight and his temper, it finally happened yesterday. And it happened at work, while I was out on a long lunch break because we were so slow. I usually take only half an hour, but yesterday I took two hours because nothing was going on. So while I was out screwing around town, my dad was spread out on the floor. The mailman was the one who found him, and I got there just as the ambulance was arriving. They don't know how long he was out, and the doctors aren't telling us much right now. He's in the hospital in the intensive care unit, and we've been able to see him for only a few minutes at a time.

My mom is hysterical, as you might imagine. I'm a little less hysterical, only because I'm trying to hold it together. He's got to pull through this or else I don't know what we're going to do. I know this is going to sound like a cliché, but I never really told him how much I care about him and respect him, or how much he's taught me, because guys don't talk that way. I've been a spoiled, whiny brat. And the last

195

thing I said to him when I left the store for my lunch break was, "Go ahead and fire me, fat man." You see, I told him I was going to take a long lunch break because I was bored stiff just standing around in an empty store. He said, "You may not have a job when you get back, lazy ass," and I said, "Go ahead and fire me, fat man." How about that for some famous last words? Or should I say that they had better not be my famous last words because I don't know how I'm going to live with that if they are. I don't think they will be—he's a tough guy and I think he'll pull through—but what if that's the last thing I say to him. I swear that if he pulls through this, I'll change. Hand on Bible.

Dorothy offered to cancel her trip home so she could come up here to be with me this weekend, but I told her not to. The person I really want to talk with is . . . you. Please take this in the spirit it is intended, but I don't know what I would ever do if something happened to you. I'm so sorry for all the stupid, jerky things I've ever said or done over the years, particularly this past year. I'm so, so sorry, Cath. You're the best friend I've ever had. So get your bony ass up here already!

Man, this sucks. The doctors and nurses barely look at us when they walk by. That can't be good, can it? Or maybe that's just the way they do their jobs.

I'll talk to you soon.

Scott

P.S. Not that it's really important in the grand scheme of things, but

I finally got the straight story from Dorothy about her grades. She really did get C's and D's, which is what she told me originally. She says she lied to you and said she got B's because she didn't want you to think she was stupid. And she says she lied to her parents and said she got straight A's because that's all she ever got before and she didn't want her parents to worry about her or pull her out of school. I guess it all makes sense, if you think about it. And, considering everything else that's going on right now, I don't really care. She's a good person, even if she's Snickers.

P.P.S. This is going to be a terrible birthday. And if my dad doesn't pull out of this soon, it will be the worst birthday in the history of mankind.

P.P.P.S. "Bony" was supposed to be funny. It was not a criticism. I am sure you have the same number of bones back there as everyone else.

He just died, Cath. Please get here as soon as you can.

Scott—

It's about 4 a.m. I woke up kind of cold on your couch, so I'm going to sneak out the basement door and go home. I'm glad we had some time to reminisce with your mom and your uncles last night. Your dad was an amazing guy. He made us laugh, even in this sad time. I'll never forget his kindness and the hard candies. And I'll never forget how much he loved you and your mom. You know that, right? He really loved you, Scott. Take a look at how happy he was in the photos from our graduation. No one can fake a smile that big.

I'm sorry I fell asleep before we finished talking about your role in the funeral. Everyone will understand if you decide that you're not comfortable speaking. Please don't stress out about that. Your idea of playing a Stones song during the ceremony is perfect. Here's my top 3 countdown from the songs you practiced last night/ this morning:

3. "Lady Jane" would be too much for your mom to bear at the funeral. Maybe save that one for after all the guests have left and you're just sitting around with family at home.

2. The sound of "Fool to Cry" was right, but the lyrics are just a little off. Your dad's Korea buddies will be hearing the words in their heads, and they don't really fit the situation.

1. "As Tears Go By" (at least the part I heard before falling asleep) was beautiful. That gets my vote.

Whatever you choose, I'll sit next to you and pretend to turn the music sheets, and we'll get through it together, okay?

See you in a few hours.

Love you,
Cath

IN TIMES OF SADNESS, KNOW THAT
YOU ARE NOT ALONE.

This was the only card I could find that didn't have a gauzy picture of a flower on the front, or of people walking in the sand. None of those seemed right for your dad.
Your father was a great man, and he will be missed.

Love,
Cath

February 16, 1983

Dear Cath,

I wanted to write a quick note and leave it in your suitcase so you'll find it when you get back to school. (Don't worry, I didn't go through your underwear. But what's the deal with the ones with the koala bears on them? You're not Australian.)

Anyway, I just wanted to thank you for being here these past few days and for helping out with everything. I know you missed some of your classes so you could stay here, and it meant a lot to me and to my mother.

And thank you for being so polite when my uncle thought that we were dating each other. He's a nice guy, but let's just say that he's not the type of guy who would understand having a girl friend who isn't a girlfriend. Anyway, you should take it as a compliment that he likes you so much.

I'm sorry I won't be there in person to say good-bye to you—again—but I have to go to the store early to open up and try to get things in order, now that I'm apparently the manager. Hooray for me, as you would say. Hooray for me.

Talk to you soon.

Thanks again.

Scott

P.S. Sorry you got stuck spending Valentine's Day here.

February 16, 1983

Dear Scott,

How are you and your mom doing?

I can't stop thinking about you and the funeral and the gathering back at your house. The fact that almost everyone in town showed up was such a huge tribute to your dad and your family. It was amazing to see so many of your parents' friends, neighbors, church members, our friends and their parents, old teachers, just about everyone from town coming out to pay their respects. It was an incredibly sad service because your dad was so young and he had so much more life to live, but it was also really inspirational to see how much people loved and respected your dad. And when all the men opened up their suit jackets to show the "Agee's Men's Clothing" labels inside? Incredible. Just incredible.

I can't even begin to understand what you're going through. There were so many things, big and small, that happened over the last few days. When I got back to school today, I got the letter that you wrote to me from the hospital. Please don't beat yourself up over the "fat man" comment. It was just banter. He'd just called you "lazy ass," and you were both kidding with each other, right? That's what people do. We've just heard so many great stories about your dad, and the common theme in all of them was that he loved to joke around. The fact that you guys were calling each other names and joking around says so much about how your relationship had changed since high school. He's gone way, way too soon, and I don't want this to come out the wrong way, but you are really lucky that you didn't go away to college. You had six months of working side by side with your dad, which you easily could have lost to writing useless term papers and drinking cheap beer and chasing sorority girls in their sweatpants. It may not feel great right now, but maybe eventually you'll like the fact that you called him "fat man" right before leaving the store for lunch.

I just can't imagine the jumble of thoughts going through your head. I mean, my head was absolutely *buzzing* the entire ride back to campus. I went straight to James's room and we went for the most amazing run this afternoon. The weather was cold and the days are just starting to get a little longer, so we just ran and ran. I was trying to process things from the weekend and the funeral, and every time I felt like crying, I just ran faster. James even said, "Damn, what have you been eating?" (And seriously, what is it with old ladies, casseroles, and deviled eggs? I've never eaten so much in my life. The truth is that I think my appetite came back because I wasn't obsessing about myself and my problems for a while. Imagine that.) I was thinking about when Todd came through the receiving line and hugged you and your mother. Despite whatever happened between Todd and your dad, you could tell how much he liked your dad. And your Uncle Bob putting his hand on your Uncle Phil's shoulder when his voice cracked and it seemed like he wouldn't be able to go on. And my dad sitting in the last pew. He didn't want to bother your mom, but I hope you know that he came to the service because he really did like and respect your dad.

And I've thought a lot about your guitar playing. "As Tears Go By" was beautiful, Scott. It was really, really beautiful. Oh, I meant to ask if one of the tunes that you played back at the house was "Um." I don't remember hearing any song with a chorus that goes, "Um um um um," though.

Write soon so I know you are doing all right, okay? I've got to get to the library to catch up on some stuff, and I have to decide if I want to start working out with the track team. This came out of left field, but James and I flew by some guys during our run today and they paced us back to our dorm. Turns out they were the assistant coaches of the girls' track team. They have spots open because there are some girls out with injuries, and they said that they were impressed by our pace. I can't lie, I was pretty flattered, and they were cool about everything, telling me that they are a fairly new Division I program, so it's not super competitive, but since I run every day anyway, why not come out and meet some of the girls? I'll have to see how it would work with my Pizza Pan hours and all that, but I'm intrigued.

Anyway, I didn't mean to go on about stupid college stuff. I'll call you soon, okay? Please write and let me know how you are doing.

Much love to you and to your mom,
Cath

P.S. Not that this is anywhere near the top of your list of things to care about right now, but Dorothy is oddly "miffed" (to use her word) about not being asked to travel to the funeral. I would not have thought that supporting a lifelong friend in a time of grief could cause jealousy, but apparently it does when dealing with a Snickers bar.

P.P.S. James asked me to tell you how sorry he was to hear about your dad. You know James. He got a little misty about it.

P.P.P.S. As for your comment in your letter about Valentine's Day, who would I rather spend it with? Other than Scott Baio or Timothy Hutton.

WAKE FOREST
UNIVERSITY

February 17, 1983

Dear Scott,

I just reread the letter you sent me from the hospital and realized
there was something that I forgot to respond to.

You're the best friend I've ever had, too.

Love,
Cath

February 20, 1983

Dear Cath,

Tell me something I don't know.

Scott

February 21, 1983

Dear Cath,

Do you ever have one of those days where you feel like you're walking through a weird dream, where nothing feels right and time seems to move in really strange ways? I feel like I've had a week of them in a row. Everything has been a blur. I know I brushed my teeth and shaved this morning because I can taste the toothpaste and my face feels relatively smooth, but I honestly have no memory of brushing my teeth or shaving. None at all. And I must have eaten breakfast and lunch, but I don't remember where I ate or what I ate. People talk to me, and I respond, but immediately afterwards, I have no idea what they said or what I said. The worst part of it is that I have no idea when this feeling will end and when everything will start feeling normal again, or if this is what normal is going to feel like. If this is now what normal feels like, it totally and completely sucks.

I'm sorry if what I'm about to say is exactly the same as what we talked about when you were here, but I really don't have any memory of what we talked about other than that you said some nice things and made me feel a little better, at least for a while. But I honestly cannot believe that I will never see my dad again. I just assumed he would always be around because, well, he always was around. He seemed like he was invincible, like nothing could kill him, like that Rasputin guy we learned

208

about in history class. My dad was shot in Korea, he was in at least two car accidents, he had gout in his left foot, his eyesight was shot, but nothing could kill him. Or that's what I thought. I always assumed that someday I'd get married and have kids, and now I'm sad to know that my dad will never get to meet my wife or my kids, and they'll never get to meet him. And I always assumed I'd do something decent with my life, and now I'm sad knowing that he's never going to see me do it. The last thing he's going to remember about me is that I was a bum who didn't go to college and was still living in his house and working in his store, and occasionally playing some bad songs on my guitar.

My mom is doing worse than she's letting on. I know she and my dad argued, a *lot* and sometimes very loudly, but they always loved each other. She says my dad was the only man she ever loved, and I think that's true. I don't know if that makes it better or worse for her. I know I'm supposed to be at home to support her, but I have to admit that I went to the movies last night instead of going home just because I didn't want to watch her crying all night. I've run out of things to say to her, and sometimes it makes me mad that we talk about how she lost her husband, but we never talk about how I lost my dad. That probably makes me a bad person, but I just couldn't do it again last night so I just went to the movies. And I couldn't even tell you what movie I saw. Seriously. I have a recollection of sitting in a movie theater, and at some point the lights went back on and I was sitting there with an empty popcorn container and an empty soda cup, and then I went home.

This Sunday, we're going to go through my dad's closet and give some of his clothes away to charity. None of it would fit me or my uncles, and it just seems like the right thing to do rather than throw it away or put it in storage. But I'm going to bet that my mom is going to change her mind and will want to keep his clothes around, at least for a while.

A lot of people have been coming by the store to say hello and pay their respects. I don't know if they're doing it to make me feel better, but they all seem to find something to buy while they're there. You'll never guess who one of the people was who came by—Donnie Dibsie. I can't say I was too excited to see him, but it ended up that he drove back from Harvard just to come to the store and pay his respects. When I thanked him and said he didn't need to do that, he said, "Of course I did—we're Tornadoes." I swear that I almost started bawling, but then he ruined the whole thing by saying, "And I'll always be your class president." What a Donnie Dipshit thing to say. But, still, it was very nice of him.

Other than the holidays, we actually had one of our biggest weeks in terms of total sales. The funny thing is that I can tell you exactly what my dad would say about that: "If I knew that would happen, I would have kicked the bucket a long time ago!" I'm counting that as the Quote of the Day even if he didn't actually say it. And if you haven't already heard, I hired Todd to come back and work at the store. I couldn't handle it on my own, and Todd already knows the routine and the merchandise. I just need to get him to understand that the employee discount is for *employees*. If it were for all the employee's friends, they would call it "the employee's friends' discount."

I'm so tired, Cath. I know I've slept off and on the past week, but I don't remember when, and it certainly doesn't feel like it.

In your letter, you mentioned that your dad showed up at the funeral. I'm sorry, but I didn't notice. I don't know whether to be surprised that he showed up or not, but please thank him for me. And thank your mom again. Please tell her that she can bake a lasagna for me again anytime she wants.

I'm glad to hear that you're going out for the track team. I don't know why you didn't think of that earlier. I'll bet you'll do well. Just don't tell anyone how much faster I am than you. And don't try arguing with me about that.

As for Dorothy being "miffed" about the funeral, I don't have the energy to even think about that, let alone analyze the way her mind works. I'm just going to apologize to her. It's much easier that way.

On the subject of girlfriends, you'll never guess who I got the nicest note from—Samantha. She knew my dad almost as well as you did, and she wrote a very nice note about how much she always liked him. Then she wrote about how badly she feels about the way she handled our breakup last fall, and how badly she feels about the way she handled things at Thanksgiving. Apparently, the guy she was dating broke up with her, and she says it made her remember how nice I always was to her—which is 94% true—and that she hopes that we can spend some time together when she comes home this summer and "see how it goes." I haven't written back to her yet because I'm not sure what I want to say. On the one hand, I want to tell her to get lost because of the way she treated me. But on the other hand, people make mistakes, and I guess you should respect it when they realize that and apologize. And on the other hand—yes, I know that's three hands—my dad always liked her and thought I was going to marry her someday, so for that reason alone I wonder if I should accept her apology and "see how it goes."

Have I mentioned how tired I am? Oh yeah, I did that a couple paragraphs ago. Sorry.

I'm going to end this letter now. I'm sure we'll talk again before you get it, but thanks again for being here to help us out. Even if I can't remember a single word you said.

Scott

P.S. Please don't tell Dorothy about Samantha's letter. I need to figure that out and don't need to get into an argument about it before I do.

P.P.S. If I did get back together with Samantha and we did get married someday, would you be my best man? I can set you up with a nice tuxedo. No employee discount, though.

P.P.P.S. My dad always liked you a lot, too, by the way. But you knew that.

Dear Scott,

I'm sorry you are going through such a sad time. I wish I knew of
some way to make it better, but I know there's nothing that I can say
that will make much of a difference right now. I just hope that eventually you'll be able to see that your dad was really proud of you. Yes,
maybe he wanted you to go to college, but when that didn't work out,
he was there for you. He trusted you with his customers and his
business, and he was grooming you to take over the store that he
built from scratch. It seems like he was very patient and loving, and
he was teaching you everything from how to measure a man for a
business suit to how to manage a rude customer. Your stories of
working with him in the store actually always reminded me of your
Boy Scout camping stories from when we were kids. Your dad was
always so calm and supportive, like that time that it was raining and
you were really struggling with the tent. He didn't just grab it from
you and do it himself or yell at you or anything, the way a lot of dads
would. He waited patiently and let you figure it out. And ever since
then, you've loved camping and basically can't shut up about how
you can pitch a tent in the rain or a strong wind or whatever. (No,
I am NOT still bitter about you having to put up my tent every time
we camped out. I think we've established that three-dimensional
assembly is not my thing. I just didn't really need to hear about it
EVERY time.)

Anyway, I think your dad had the same attitude about you

working in the store. He probably hoped that you would eventually love it and take great pride in it if he just sat back and let you do it for yourself, as much as possible. The most important thing though, Scott, is that he loved you and he wanted you to be happy. Please try not to be so down on yourself. I really believe that is the last thing that your dad would have wanted. Of course, I'm sure he never expected to pass away at such a young age. If he had been ill or something like that, I'm sure he would have told you over and over again how much he loved you and how proud he was of you. He just didn't have the chance.

I'm also sorry that your mom is having such a hard time. I talked to my mom, and she and some of the other neighborhood ladies are going to make more of an effort to stop by and spend time with your mom. It must be a terrible shock to her to lose your dad like that, with no warning or anything. I just keep thinking how full of life and energy he was. It is hard to comprehend that he's really gone.

You know, I was thinking that maybe my mom could help you out at the store. You and I haven't had much time to talk about her lately, and there are much more important things to talk about right now, but she seems to have turned a corner and is doing so much better than she was over the holidays. Even with all the sadness and emotion of your dad's funeral last week, she's not drinking at all. When I asked her about it, she said that's just not who she is, or who she wants to be. She said that it's still hard to accept that my dad left her for a younger woman, but she is trying to see it as an opportunity for a fresh start. She's been getting rave reviews at the card store, and they promoted her to assistant manager, which means she makes a little more money. And she joined a "Jazzercise" class. I don't really know what that is. It sounds kind of like the Jane Fonda tapes that the girls on my hall do, but she "love-love-loves it" and has a mini wardrobe of leotards and braided headbands hanging in the laundry room to prove it. Anyway, if you need a more mature salesperson to supervise Todd, or just to help you in general, you might want to talk to her.

Oh boy, and now we get to Samantha. Wow. I mean, wow. The good thing is that there's no rush, right? She's away at the Unaccredited Virginia School for the Clueless, and you probably can't see her until summer break because of work, so it's not like you have to make a decision right now. You're dealing with a lot of stuff right now, so, yeah, I'm glad she sent you a nice note and all. You should do whatever you want, obviously, but this probably isn't a great time to rush into anything, you know? It's nice that your dad liked her so much. I have to wonder, though, did you tell him about what happened at Thanksgiving? Sorry if you don't want me to remind you, but that was pretty shitty. Anyway, whatever, let's not get crazy and start talking about marriage, assuming you were even halfway serious about that. I mean, I know your dad just passed away and you're thinking a lot of Big Thoughts these days, but we're only 18, right? Maybe you should just slow it down a bit, in general? There's so much history with Samantha. Some of it is good history, but there's some bad stuff to consider, as well, right?

And don't worry, I won't say anything to Dorothy. I hardly see her these days anyway, and I'll make sure she doesn't see your latest letter.

Given all the important things going on these days, I won't bore you today with my chatter about the track team and whatnot. We've got plenty of time for all of that.

I miss you, and I hope things get better soon.

Love,
Cath

P.S. I just remembered that you're 19 now, although that was a birthday we'd all like to forget.

P.P.S. I almost cried when I heard that Donnie Dibsie came back to pay his respects. He's a good guy. Let's not make fun of him anymore, okay? After all, we're all Tornadoes.

February 28, 1983

Dear Cath,

I'm sorry I missed your call last night. I've been working around the clock. I didn't get home until almost one in the morning because I had to stick around after we closed to count the money in the cash register—then recount it, then recount it *again* because it didn't add up right. Then I had to restack the clothes on the shelves and do inventory, and then I had to fill out order forms, and then I had to send out checks to our suppliers. And then I had to turn right around this morning to do it all over again. I have never been so tired in my life. Never. I feel like I've just run 100 miles, entirely uphill. I honestly have no idea how adults do this every day of the week, week in and week out. And I have no idea how my dad figured out how to get everything done in time to get home by seven o'clock for dinner. I mean, that cash register alone took me three hours. I know I'm not the smartest guy in the world, but each time I counted the drawer, I came up with a completely different number—and none of those numbers matched up with the number on the tape. If it were just a couple cents, I'd forget about it. But how could it be off by ten or twenty dollars each time? How?

Anyway, I'm tired. Very, very tired.

And I wish I were in college, like you and everyone else we know, but I'm not.

Do you remember that time junior year when I had to take a couple days off school to go to Baltimore to get my eyes checked? Well, it was a lie. Or half a lie. After my parents told him about how I have trouble spelling and with math, Dr. Grossman—Chris's dad—told me he thought I might have this thing called "dyslexia." It's this thing where your brain mixes up letters and numbers. So he made an appointment for me to see a doctor at Johns Hopkins Hospital in Baltimore to take a bunch of tests. That's when I told you I was going to get my eyes checked. My parents were actually excited about it because they figured if it was some medical issue, we could get it fixed, and then I'd turn into a straight-A student and go off to college. Anyway, the tests took all day, and then I had to go back to Baltimore on another day to get the results. The doctor sat me down like he was going to tell me I had some terminable disease. Then he said, "Scott, I wish I could make this simpler for you, but you don't have dyslexia." I don't? "No, you don't. I wish I could give you an answer, but I think the answer may just be that you're bad at spelling." And math? "And math. It's probably just that you don't try hard enough. You're kind of what we call an underachiever."

Hmm, where have I heard that before?

So I actually have a medical opinion that I'm an underachiever.

Do you know what's sad—I was actually hoping he'd tell

me I had "dyslexia" because I wouldn't have to take responsibility. And I know my parents were thinking the same thing. But not going to college is all on me, isn't it?

And underachiever or not, I can't run the store by myself. I just can't do it. I'm going to stop by your house tomorrow to see if your mom wants to come work at the store a couple days a week. (I don't know if I mentioned it or not, but my mom is going to come in a few days a week, too.)

And I have to tell Farrah that he's out of the band and Todd's back in, which Farrah will not take well.

And I just broke up with Dorothy over the phone, which I'm sure you've heard about nonstop ever since it happened. I probably should have called you ahead of time to warn you so you could hide, but it just sort of happened naturally in the course of the conversation. Before you tell me that I should have broken up with her in person like a gentleman, my mother has already said that exact same thing. I agree that would have been the best way to do it. But I don't know when I would see her in person again. It could be months, and I didn't feel like pretending or dragging this out. She's a good person, but she was driving me nuts. I just remembered what my dad used to call her. Everything was so dramatic with her. If I liked drama, I'd go see *The Godfather*.

As for Samantha, well, I know you and she don't exactly like each other, but I'm still crazy about her, Cath. I've been crazy about her since the first time I met her after her family moved here. I know you think the only reason I dated her is because she's blond and pretty and looks great in a bikini, but that's not true at all. She's also very sweet, and she gets my jokes, and if I had to list the 100 nicest things anyone has ever said to me, 50 would be from her. (Of the remaining 50, 25 would be from my mom, and 25 would be from you.) I know she treated me like crap when she went off to college, and I haven't forgotten what happened at Thanksgiving. But if someone you care about apologizes to you, if someone you've held in your arms tells you that she's so sorry for what she did, shouldn't you accept that apology? I mean, people make mistakes, right? And if you can't forgive someone you're close to for making a mistake, then why do apologies even exist?

This is a long way of saying that I've accepted Samantha's apology and I like having her back in my life again and looking at her picture before I go to sleep. If I can ever get away from work, I may try to go visit her in the next couple weeks, and she says she may be able to come home during her spring break. And she'll also be back for the summer. Whatever happens happens. If nothing happens, I'll be fine. But if I end up getting back together with the only girl who's ever loved me, you won't hear me complaining. And if we do get back together, I will have to figure out how to convince you and her to get along. I still don't understand what the issue is you have with each other. I mean, you're both great people. And one of you is an amazing kisser.

Okay, now I feel bad. I'm talking about kissing Samantha when my dad died and I should be thinking about him. Now I'm remembering how tired he was when he got home from work. All he wanted to do after dinner was lie on the couch and watch TV, and I used to complain that he was too lazy to go outside and shoot baskets with me. But now I get why he was so tired every night. And now I realize what a complete shit I was.

I'm going to go to sleep now. I have to get up in few hours. Good luck dealing with Dorothy.

Talk to you soon.

Scott

MARCH

March 2, 1983

Dear Scott,

I hope you don't mind, but I've been talking to Jane about you and your dad and everything. I've been kind of lucky so far in my life and haven't had anyone that I'm close to pass away, but Jane has some experience with it, and it's been nice for me to be able to talk to her. She said that all the fatigue that you're feeling is really typical for someone who is grieving. She said that she remembers feeling like she was living two lives at the same time—one in the past, where her new understanding of loss made her see so many interactions from the past in a different light, and one in the present, where she was fighting to keep it together on a daily basis. She said she can't imagine how hard it must be for you to also have the responsibility of working in the store, on top of everything. Jane's advice was to just listen to your body, as much as you possibly can. Don't feel bad if you sleep all day on your day off or call the band to blow off practice so you can lie on the couch. She said our society sucks at supporting a grieving person and you just have to take care of yourself and hope that people cut you some slack. On the other hand, if you're suddenly having a good day, don't beat yourself up about it. She said that she used to worry that she would forget her mom if she didn't think about her all the time, but she swears, Scott, that your dad will stay with you, in lots of good and happy ways, and you don't have to stay sad to remember him. Anyway, if you ever want to talk to someone who really gets what

224

you're going through, Jane's here and she'd be happy to talk to you, okay?

You know, I do get the whole Samantha thing. In a way, I may even get it more than you do, because I can see it. In 3-D. Everyone can see it. You're a completely different person around her, and you always have been. And I get it. And it's cool. And I don't mean to be unsupportive. It's just that Samantha's just a little bit careless, you know? When I think of Samantha, I think of her driving too fast with the windows down, her long hair blowing all over the place, tunes cranked, soda in hand, laughing her ass off about something you just said. And that's cool. It's all good, really. But, you know, I can't help but worry about you, Scott. I'm worried that she's going to hurt you again. Okay. There. I've said it. I'm sure I've said too much, and I'll shut up now and like you said, whatever happens, happens. And you know, Scott, I really do want you to be happy, and if you get back together with Samantha and she makes you happy, then I promise to try not to worry so much and to be nicer about everything.

Oh, and by the way, don't worry about Dorothy. She's found a big bony shoulder to cry on, which belongs to . . . James! (You didn't think I was going to say Walter, did you?) How did we not see this coming? She loves drama. He's a big old softy. *Et voilà!*—they can't get enough of each other. It's sweet, actually, and they seem to really click together.

Anyway, Jane and I have both cut our hours way back at the Pizza Pan so she can do all her sorority pledge stuff and I can work out with the track team.

225

And I'm totally loving being on the track team. I have to say, I didn't get the whole sorority thing before. Like, how could you have a couple of cocktail parties, meetings, and events, and suddenly you're all wearing the same sweatshirts and being best friends? I was pretty cynical about it, and I thought it was really fake and surfacy. But now I sort of get it. I mean, I've only been working out with the track girls for a few weeks, and I feel like I've made some really good friends. (Katie, Donna, Sandy, and Donna-with-the-Headbands, so we don't confuse her with the other Donna.) We're together in the gym or on the track for about two hours every afternoon. They're a very cool, very funny group. The coaches think I'll be better at cross-country than track, and right now I am working on overall speed and endurance. Even though I have a lot to learn and most of the girls are way faster than I am, I love it. I love wearing official athletic department practice gear and sweatshirts. I love being with so many other girls who love to run. I love hanging around the athletic complex with the other spring athletes. Need I remind you of how I feel about baseball players? Probably not.

I really like the coaches, too. They've been helpful in teaching me about nutrition as well as running. No wonder I couldn't sleep through the night! I was jazzed on caffeine and hungry all the time. Since joining the team, I've been eating better and sleeping through the night again, which is awesome.

My parents are really happy about the track team thing, too, although my dad keeps reminding me that I have to come home for Spring Break and have to miss any meets that are scheduled that week because The Baby will be arriving. (As if I could forget.) And my mom has probably worn out her welcome at the store, bragging about me. Sorry about that. She's always been the president of my fan club.

Other than that, how is it working out having our moms helping you at the store? If you need any help while I'm home for Spring Break, I'd be happy to work the cash register or fold clothes at the end of the day, or whatever. It would be great to spend time with you and not to have to spend the entire break either waiting for The Baby to arrive or changing its diapers.

Okay, I guess I can't put off studying for midterms any longer. I'll call you soon. I hope you are getting a lot of sleep and things are getting a little better.

Love,
Cath

P.S. I forgot to mention that I'm so excited that Todd is back in the band! With the van back, does that mean you can travel to play shows? I put "Have a Heart" on the team warm-up tape, and everyone loves it. Just let me know if you want to talk to the manager at the Pizza Pan about scheduling a gig. He still asks about you when he sees the sticker on my backpack.

March 5, 1983

Dear Cath,

That was nice of you to suggest I talk with your friend Jane. She's the one with the black hair, right? I'm sure she's a very nice person and all, but I'm going to pass. I'm all talked out these days, and I don't feel like talking to someone I don't know anyway. What's the point? Most people don't even want to talk about me or my dad. Instead, after saying they're sorry, everyone wants to tell me about how they know exactly what I'm going through because someone they knew died, too, as if that's supposed to make me feel better. I get it—lots and lots of people die. Great. Thanks a lot. I just don't need to hear about someone else's grandmother or mailman who died, or their grandmother's mailman, or their mailman's grandmother, or whoever the hell they want to talk about who died. And I don't want to hear about how this person died of cancer, and that person died in a car accident, and that other person died from the bubonic plague. I'm sorry they all died, okay? And I'm sure whatever they died of was terrible. But I don't want to hear about it.

Here's another thing I don't want to hear about: how my dad should've taken better care of himself. (I almost wrote "should of" taken better care of himself—can you imagine what Mrs. Anki would say about that?) They all say, "Your dad was a great guy. We're really going to miss him. Blah, blah, blah." Then, eventually, they all say, "I wish he'd taken better care of himself."

228

I can't tell you how many people have said that to me. Or, "What happened to your dad is a lesson for all of us about how important it is to take care of ourselves." Look, I understand what they're trying to say, but it's still a crappy thing to say. It doesn't change anything. It's like they're blaming him or saying it's his own fault. Maybe it was. But why the hell do you think I want to hear you say that?

I'm sorry if this isn't a particularly good letter. I'm so tired from work, even with everyone helping me out. It could be worse. If my dad hadn't been so well organized, I would have no idea how to run this store. He had folders for everything. Maybe if he hadn't made so many folders, he would have taken better care of himself, right? Right.

I'm glad to hear things are going well at school and with the track team. Maybe I'll come down to see one of your meets, if you tell me when they are—and if you promise that Dorothy and James won't be there. The thought of those two making out might make me throw up. And the thought of throwing up makes me want to throw up more.

If I do come down, maybe I'll bring the band with me and we'll play at that pizza place where you work. And do you have any idea how much they'll pay us? Tell your boss we usually get paid $10,000 a show, but we'll give them a discount and do it for $50 and some pizza. And beer. And not the cheap beer, either.

Speaking of the band, Farrah stopped by the store today, and I told him he's out of the band and that Todd is back in. I ended up being completely wrong about the guy. I thought he was going to go crazy when I told him he's out of the band, but he couldn't have been cooler. He told me that he knew I was going through a tough time, that he understood that Todd had been the original drummer, that it would be wrong for him not to give the drummer's seat back to Todd, and that I should call him if Todd was ever unavailable or if I just wanted to hang out and jam. The way he handled the whole thing made me feel good and bad at the same time, if you know what I mean. But then he started telling me about how he knew what I was going through because his uncle died, and I wanted to tell him to shut . . . the . . . hell . . . up.

The Moms have been a big help at the store. No kidding. They talk a lot about your dad and my dad. And about us. What a surprise. Apparently, neither of us knows anything about what love is.

Speaking of which, Samantha sent me a long letter. It was a very nice letter, that's all I'll say. I'm looking forward to seeing her when she comes home for spring break. I know you'll be home at the same time. Maybe we can all get together for dinner or lunch or something.

I'll talk to you soon.

Scott

March 8, 1983

Dear Scott,

I'm so excited that you're willing to play at the Pizza Pan! Hooray for
us! I'm going to have my manager call you at the store this week.
His name is Billy Thorn. The band that he had scheduled to play on
St. Patrick's Day just canceled on him for a higher-paying gig, so
he'll really want you guys to come down. I mean, wait, that didn't
come out right. That's not the only reason he'll want you. Billy has
liked Crush since he heard your tape last semester, and he's wanted
you to play all along.

This will be great! It's the Thursday before we all leave for
Spring Break, and Billy says it usually gets pretty wild. I hope it isn't
too soon for you, you know, after your dad and everything. Will it
be good to have something fun to look forward to, though? I hope
so because you deserve to be happy.

Anyway, I have to run because we have a meet this afternoon.
I'm not running an event, but I'm still really excited to be there as
an alternate and to wear my shiny new tracksuit and everything.
I'm going to drop this at the post office and go by the Pizza Pan
right now to leave Billy a note with your phone number on it. Make
my mom cover your shifts if you have to. You're the boss now, and
she says she likes chatting with all the men who come into the
store anyway. (I was sort of creeped out to hear that, but who can
blame her?)

Much love,
Cath

P.S. I also might be a little bit excited because the girls' track team has a mixer with the baseball team this Thursday night and, in case I forgot to mention it, I'm on the girls' track team. And, yeah, well, there's the baseball player part, too.

March 10, 1983

Dear Cath,

I just spoke with Billy, and we're all set for the gig at the Pizza Pan. It should be fun. Maybe it'll be the start of a worldwide tour of pizza parlors. The Moms are going to handle the store for themselves for Thursday and Friday, so that's covered. The only problem is that we need to find a place to sleep that Thursday night. If we stay in a hotel, we'll wind up losing money on the trip. And as much as I'm sure you'd love to have us all sleeping on the floor of your dorm room, there's the Dorothy problem. (Remind me to use that as a title for a song: "The Dorothy Problem.") If you have any ideas about where we could sleep, please let me know. Otherwise, we'll be sleeping in Todd's van. (Remind me to buy some air fresheners for the trip.)

Thanks for all the nice things you said. They mean a lot. And thanks for reminding me that you're on the track team. I had almost forgotten it since the last time you mentioned it. And thanks for reminding me about your general attraction to baseball players. It's the tight pants, isn't it? Come on, admit it.

Speaking of admitting things, I have something to admit to you. Remember last fall when my dad wanted to know what your SAT scores were? When I told him, he said, "You're 80% as smart as she is, I'll bet you could get 1400 if you tried." I didn't tell you this for a lot of reasons, but he got me some SAT prep books and he signed me up for the SATs. I actually read the

233

books because, well, there was nothing else to do at night with everyone off at college already, and I took the test on a Saturday morning with most of the current senior class of East Bloomfield High. The scores came in the mail last fall, and let's just say I'm not 80% as smart as you. It's closer to 95%. Don't laugh, but somehow I got 1500 out of 1600, including 780 on English. Yes, *English*. So I was thinking about maybe applying to colleges, but then a lot of stuff happened and I missed the deadlines, so I figured I would wait to apply until next year. But the past few weeks, my mom started talking about how proud my dad would be if I went to college, and how she knew that I felt trapped here now and she didn't want me to feel trapped. I told her I'd already missed the deadlines, so she called up a bunch of schools, explained that my dad had just died, and asked if they could make an exception for me and let me apply after the deadline had passed. Believe it or not, she actually talked five schools into letting me apply late, including Samantha's. Anyway, I just sent off five college applications. They gave me only a few days to send in my applications, so instead of writing an essay, I just included the lyrics to "Daddy Issues," along with a tape of the song. I figure that, at the very least, it will be different.

I hope you're not mad that I didn't mention the SATs before, but hopefully the fact that you're 5% smarter than me makes up for that. I'll let you know as soon as I hear anything. Samantha's excited about the possibility that I might be going to college with her next year, if I can get in. I am, too. But I'm trying not to get too excited. If I don't get into any of the schools, I'll be right here, selling men's clothing with the Moms and Todd. That's okay, too, I guess.

Okay, I have to get back to work. In case you were wondering, while the Moms are doing a good job around here, they could do more work if they stopped talking to each other all day. Seriously, it's nonstop. I'm surprised they still have vocal cords. And before I forget, the Moms also convinced Todd to get a haircut. They told him he has a beautiful face and he "shouldn't hide his light under a bushel." I have no idea what that means, but wait until you see it. I would send a photo, but I don't have one. Let me just say two words instead: Dorothy Hamill.

Talk to you soon, college girl.

Scott, maybe a college guy

P.S. It is the tight pants, isn't it? I knew it.

March 13, 1983

Dear Scott,

You took the SATs last fall and didn't tell me about it? You weasel! I tell you everything, and you don't tell me about *that*! That's huge news, Scott!

I'm so excited that you applied to college for next year! I've always known that you are much smarter than your grades reflected. That's so great, Scott. I'm really happy for you. You're going to love being away from home and hanging with teenagers instead of old people all the time. When will you hear back from all your schools?

I'm also really excited to see Crush on St. Patty's Day. I have a big paper due Thursday and I'll be totally psyched to party after I hand it in. Don't stress about where you guys will sleep. This is college! Sleeping arrangements are pretty flexible. Bowl haircut or no bowl haircut, Todd will be snuggled up with some little cutie somewhere, and if worse comes to worst, the rest of you can crash on my guy friends' floors or on the couches in the commons room. James has a single, so Dorothy will probably stay at his place that night, and you could maybe even stay in my room. Don't worry, it will all work out. And if it doesn't, you may have a jump start on the lyrics to "The Dorothy Problem."

Now let's just hope that The Baby stays where it is until after Thursday. I talked to my dad today and he is a nervous wreck. Apparently, Amanda went into "false labor" last night and they rushed her to the hospital, only to be sent back home. (And, apparently, the secretary has a name—and apparently, it's "Amanda.") I have to admit, now that we are so close to The Baby being born, I am sort of looking forward to it. It's kind of cool that I'll be a big sister. The closest I've had to a little brother or sister has been Plum.

I'm off to the library to start my research paper. Can't wait to see you in a few days! I'll grab a ride home with you guys in the van on Friday, okay? And I'll bring some air fresheners!

Much love,
Cath

P.S. No, it's not just the pants. It's the beauty of so many moments during a game. And the pants.

P.P.S. Unfortunately, as I learned at the mixer a few nights ago, most of the players also have beautiful girlfriends. Not pretty—beautiful. Maybe I should follow Jane's lead and go for a soccer player. If only I could get over the feeling that I'm looking at them in a fun house mirror, with their skinny chests and tree trunk legs. See, it's these types of intense thoughts that you'll have to grapple with if you go to college next year. I'm pretty sure you'll be able to handle it!

Dear Scott,

That.
Was.
A.
Mazing!

You guys were awesome! You completely ROCKED! I mean, I'm at a loss for words. It was incredible.

And, oh my God, when you pulled me up onstage to sing the chorus of "You Don't Know Me"—that was otherworldly. I've never felt like that in my life. I was nervous at first, but then it felt like I was floating. I hope I did the song justice. But now I totally understand the high you get when you're up onstage singing your songs.

Anyway, amazing.

Absolutely amazing.

Looking forward to hanging out.

Love,
Cath

March 20, 1983

Cath—

Sorry I haven't seen you much since we got back to town, but Samantha is keeping me very busy when I'm not at the store, if you know what I mean.

I wanted to thank you again for setting up the gig at the Pizza Pan. Man, that was fantastic! Not to brag, but WE ROCKED! We totally and completely ROCKED! And you were great singing on "You Don't Know Me."

Let's catch up after I drive Samantha back to school next weekend.

Enjoy the rest of your spring break, and let me know when the baby arrives.

Scott

March 23, 1983

Dear Cath,

I wish I could say that our call tonight was the worst phone call I've ever had, but I had an even worse one with Samantha right afterwards. Maybe you and Samantha should talk because as much as you both dislike each other, you both seem to agree that I'm a jerk.

Anyway, I'm sorry if I didn't handle things well, or if the words didn't come out right. But Samantha wasn't happy to find out that I drove down to play at Wake, or that I slept in your room, even though Joe did, too, and she wasn't too happy that you drove back with us in Todd's van. That's all I was trying to say to you. I was hoping you'd give me some advice or tell me that everything was going to be okay. I probably should have remembered the Samantha Rules and not talked with you about her at all. I'm sorry.

I don't want to fight with you about this, Cath. I don't. And everything you said makes sense, even the part about how I'm being stupid and a jerk. When I called Samantha back and tried to repeat what you had said, about how we've been friends forever, it actually made things worse and she started crying.

She said, "How am I supposed to compete with that?"

And I said, "Compete with what?"

240

And she said, "How am I supposed to compete with some-one you've been friends with forever?"

And I said, "There's no competition, Sam. She's my friend. You're my girlfriend."

And she said, "Don't be so sure about that."

And I said, "What does that mean?"

And she said, "Exactly what you think." She was crying, and I kept trying to calm her down, then she said, "I have a question, and I want you to answer it honestly. I deserve hon-esty."

And I said, "Go ahead."

And she said, "I want an honest answer. Have you ever cheated on me with Cath? Don't lie. Tell me the truth."

And I said, "Never."

And she said, "Cross your heart."

And I said, "Absolutely. I've never cheated on you with Cath. I've never cheated on you with anyone." I almost said, "Unlike you. You cheated on me, remember?" but I didn't.

But then she said, "Do you think she's pretty? Don't lie. You think she's pretty, don't you?"

And I said, "Yes."

She laughed and said, "Thank you for being honest, I guess. But I wish you'd lied." And then she said, "Have you ever kissed her?"

I paused for a second because of that kiss at Duffy's, and when I didn't answer right away, she went berserk. She said, "I knew it! I knew it all along! You two were making out the whole time we were dating in high school, weren't you?"

I told her no, and I tried to calm her down, even when she was calling me names, and I explained what happened at Duffy's, that it was completely meaningless, that you'd meant to kiss me on the cheek, etc.

When I told her the waitress at Duffy's kissed me, too, she said, "What the fuck? Are you making out with everyone in that dumb-ass town?" Then she said, "You talked to her tonight before you called me, didn't you?"

I said, "Who? The waitress?" thinking I could make a joke out of the whole thing.

And she said, "No, Catherine Fucking Osteen."

And I said, "Her middle name's Evelyn, after her grandmother."

And she said, "I couldn't give a flying fuck what Catherine Osteen's middle name is or how she fucking got it. I want to know if you talked with Catherine Fucking Osteen tonight before you called me."

When I told her I had, she said she wanted me to promise that I wouldn't talk to you anymore. Ever. I didn't agree to that. I told her that wasn't fair and that we can talk about it some more when I visit her this weekend. But as long as Samantha and I are still dating, I have to think about her and what she wants. So, if it's okay with you, I think we need to cool it with the phone calls and letters for a bit.

And I'm going to assume that's cool with you since, as of
a couple hours ago, you thought I was a complete asshole.

Okay?

Love,
Scott

Dear Scott,

I'm sorry I didn't handle things well on that call either. I don't think that you're an asshole or a jerk. It just really frosts me to have to deal with your jealous girlfriend. I mean, come on, you and I have been friends forever and we've had so much going on in our lives lately, of course we need to talk to each other. We're connected. I'm sorry if that freaks Samantha out, but it is what it is. And I'm not going to "cool it" with writing to you because you are off visiting Samantha at the Virginia College for Morons and Skanks right now and how else could I tell you that I HAVE A BABY SISTER!

Oh, Scott, she's the most beautiful thing in the world. And she looks right into my eyes when I hold her and talk to her. I'm really surprised, but I love her so much already. She's so beautiful, and I think she knows that I'm her big sister. She calms down when I hold her, except when she's hungry, but that's another story. And one that you'll like because it involves boobs.

But anyway, I've been on the craziest emotional roller coaster tonight. I wish you were here! I really need one of our late nights where I pace around your basement as you sort of, maybe, half listen to me as I ramble about everything that has just happened, and I throw things at you if you fall asleep. No more ashtrays, I promise, I know that left a mark, but you know, pencils, shoes, pillows, whatever, I need to throw some stuff at you right now! My heart and my head are racing like the bass line in "Mystery Achievement." Or maybe it's the drum line. Whatever, you know what I mean. Chrissie Hynde is such a badass.

So the delivery was *nuts*. I was over at my dad's place when Amanda's water broke. She was cool as a cucumber, but my dad lost his mind. He was in such a panic that he threw the car keys into the backseat and tried to stick his glasses in the ignition. Amanda convinced him to sit in the backseat with her and to let me drive them to over to Cedar Creek Hospital. Thank God you taught me how to drive your little piece-of-shit Honda last summer! The clutch on the Mercedes was harder to work than yours, but I got used to it pretty quickly. Anyway, everything calmed down a lot when we got to the hospital, and my dad and I mostly hung out in the waiting room while they got Amanda settled. I was struggling with so many things. I was trying not to think about how it was that we ended up there in the first place, with my dad's girlfriend about to have a baby, and feeling horrible about having to call my mom to explain why I would be late getting home, and scared for Amanda, and really excited and nervous to see the baby. Before long they called my dad back to the delivery room, and then the nurse came to get me. I walked in there expecting to see a Norman Rockwell painting, and instead it looked like a crime scene! Holy shitballs! There was blood, and there were too many people, and my dad was laid out on a gurney like a dead man. I got dizzy, and a nurse sat me in a chair and said, "I guess it runs in the family." Long story short, back when I was born, they apparently didn't bring dads into the delivery room until after the baby was born. These days, they bring them in for the big event, and even ask the dads if they want to cut the umbilical cord. (WHAT?) Well, my dad was NOT prepared for that, and he passed out cold in the middle of everything! When I saw him on the gurney, I thought about your dad and everything that you'd been through in that exact same hospital. I'm so sorry, Scott, I know it's unfair, but I cried with relief when my dad woke up. I'm not strong enough to go through what you are going through, and Amanda looked so young and helpless with the little infant in her arms, and I kept thinking, "What is she going to do without my dad to take care of them?"

We all had a good laugh at my dad's expense when he woke up, and then we did a lot of gazing at the baby, and holding the baby, and learning about swaddling the baby, and then staring at her some more. By the way, I am still referring to my sister as "the baby" because Amanda and my dad can't agree on a name. Amanda is rock solid when it comes to having a baby, as it turns out, but she's still a little bit of a dummy when it comes to naming a baby, and she wants a name like "Bianca" or "Chantelle." I don't really care, as long as it's not something that other kids can tease her about when she grows up, like "Patty Patty Fo Fatty" or whatever. She's so beautiful, she will make almost any name perfect.

Whew, I just realized that I'm exhausted. If you were here, you would get up off the couch at this point, walk me across the street and help me get my head straight about what to say to my mom in the morning. But you're not here, so I'll just have to figure that out on my own. Thanks a lot, Samantha.

246

I'll be home all summer. I'm going to babysit for my sister after Amanda goes back to work. Maybe your girlfriend will chill out by then and we can hang out like normal. You have to get to know the baby. You're practically her uncle. No, wait, her brother. Whatever, it's 3:30 in the morning. It's too hard to think right now.

I miss you. And this is crazy, but I miss my no-named sister already, too.

Love,
Catherine Fucking Osteen

P.S. As far as the recent Samantha drama goes, the less we say about it, the better.

March 29, 1983

Dear Cath,

I couldn't find a "Congratulations on the Birth of Your Sister" card anywhere in the card shop. Maybe if I write "Hallmark" at the bottom of this letter, that will make it official.

So, congratulations on the birth of your sister! Very cool!

Your mom told my mom about it at work—I don't want to even think about how that conversation went—so I knew about it before I got your letter. I had no idea you would be so excited about it. I mean, I know how messy and difficult everything has been for you, and I know you weren't that thrilled with the whole situation, but I'm glad to see that you're excited. However you may feel about your dad and his secretary—I noticed you actually called her by her name!—I guess that shouldn't affect the way you feel about your sister. It's not like she had anything to do with it.

Anyway, I suspect you've talked with your mom and know how freaked out she is about this whole thing. You might want to give her a call or send her a nice letter or something because she's afraid she's going to get pushed out of your life now and that you're going to spend all your time with your dad, the secretary, and the baby. She didn't tell me that directly, but it's a pretty good summary of the conversation the Moms were having with Todd at work today. Yes, the Moms talk about stuff like that with Todd. The weirdest part is that he seems to enjoy it. He even gives them both advice sometimes, and he reads the articles they cut out for him from *Redbook*. Deep down, he may be a 50-year-old woman. Who plays the drums and can't get to work on time.

I know you don't want to hear about my trip to visit Samantha at her school, which is *not* called the Virginia College for Morons and Skanks, at least not according to the brochures, so I won't say anything about it other than that it was okay. Not perfect, not great, but okay. A little weird, maybe. I'm sure that's natural since it's the first time I've visited her there, and I didn't know any of her friends or anything. But that will be different if I'm at school there with her next year. Or should I say *when* I'm at school there next year. I just found out I got in. (It's the only acceptance I got.) I'm very excited. I'm going to go to college after all. My dad would be proud.

What else can I tell you?

Work's good.

We're setting up a few more gigs for the band. I'm completely reworking the lyrics for "Um." I wanted to make it a little more personal. Maybe I'll send the new lyrics to you when I finish them up. We almost have enough original songs now that we could make an album. Not that I'm saying we're going to do that, just that we could.

And if we want to do that, we'd better hurry since Todd may be going through menopause soon. (I had never heard about "menopause" until the Moms started talking about it at work. It's on the long list of things the Moms don't think any of us understand.)

I'm going to head to bed now. I hope you have enjoyed this card.

Take care. And "Congratulations on the Birth of Your Sister."

Scott

P.S. Baseball season is about to start. Go Orioles!

HALLMARK

APRIL

Dear Scott,

Way to go, college boy!

I'm so proud of you going to college, and I know your dad would be even prouder.

Wow!

Scott Agee is going to college!

Of course, I won't actually be able to visit him there because of his jealous skank of a girlfriend, but still, wow! I mean, wow! Hooray for you!

Before I start talking all about me again, I have to tell you that I thought about your family and your dad so much during this past Easter weekend. I don't go to church very often anymore, but I did go on Easter, and I was so overwhelmed with memories of all those years that we shared Easter egg hunts and made fun of each other for having to get so dressed up for Mass. And memories of our dads, especially your dad. My dad volunteering to have our family bring up the gifts when you were serving on the altar, and your dad giving me such a pleased look as we made our way back to the pew. I don't know if I've told you often enough, Scott, but I really do miss your dad. I think about him and about you and your mom a lot and I hope you know that I'm here for you if you ever need to talk about him.

Anyway, it's time to start talking about ME again.

On Monday, I got my courage up and asked a sophomore guy that I work with to go to our dorm formal with me. You met him briefly during your St. Patty's Day gig. His name's Andrew. Anyway, I was so awkward. You would have laughed your ass off if you'd seen it. My voice was quivering, and I think that at least one eye and maybe my whole face was twitching as I asked him. Fortunately, he quickly said yes, probably just to keep me from going into a full-blown seizure. I was drenched in sweat for the rest of our shift together. I almost put my poetry notebook in the pizza oven and had to walk around outside to get my hands to stop shaking. Seriously, how do boys ask girls out all the time? It is so hard! (Insert lame sex joke here.)

When I told my mom about it on the phone, she insisted on bringing me a new dress and taking me to lunch as an early birthday present. Given that she's been upset about my plan to babysit Jennifer this summer—if you haven't heard, the baby's name is "Jennifer Crystalle," and yes, I'm doing my best to ignore the "Crystalle" part—I couldn't really say no, even though I had a big paper due on Thursday. Anyway, I have to admit, my mom brought me a really pretty dress, and we had a great talk for about the first hour of lunch. She got more comfortable with my plan to babysit this summer when I explained my thinking—that it will be a great way to spend time with my sister while not having to deal with Amanda, who will be at work whenever I am with Jennifer. Mom also agrees that the baby is going to need me to read to her and talk to her in a normal voice and help her not to become some wacky little hair-sprayed princess, given that her mother is such a wacky big hair-sprayed princess. Mom also likes the idea of keeping the babysitting money in the family, since we're all a little tight on cash. (That's not a criticism of how much she's being paid to work at the store.) We also visited the Financial Aid Office while my mom was here, and they were really helpful. I don't think I told you this, but my dad has been pressuring me to transfer to the University of Maryland for the in-state tuition. My mom knows how much I love it here at Wake, so she's been helping me fill out all the forms to get into the work-study program, and the track coaches have told the Financial Aid Office that they're holding a spot for me on the cross-country team next fall, so we're going to cobble together some different sources of funds to keep me here next year.

Speaking of money, do you think you could put in a good word for me at Duffy's? I've gotten some good bartending and food service experience this year, and I bet the weekend and night shift waitresses get good tips there, especially when Crush is playing.

Speaking of Crush, I don't understand how you can have almost enough original songs for an album! You've been holding out on me! I've only heard "Daddy Issues," "Sometimes, Jeanie Blue," "You Don't Know Me," and "Have a Heart." I still haven't heard "Um" or seen the lyrics to it. Please send them to me. And please send me a tape of your new stuff. Jane and I will listen to it and give you our unvarnished, First Official Crush Groupies' opinion.

But I digress, because I haven't told you about the second hour of my lunch with my mother. Or rather, perhaps there's something that YOU have not been telling ME.

Who the hell is this "Chris Caldwell" character?

If she said "Chris Caldwell" once, she said it a hundred times.

"Chris Caldwell" is an old high school friend of hers who has, "You know, been on the annual Christmas card list." (No. I didn't know.)

"Chris Caldwell" recently got a big promotion and got transferred to his firm's Baltimore office.

"Chris Caldwell" has been shopping at Agee's Clothes, where men and boys shop, to update his wardrobe, "You know, because of the big promotion and all."

Despite the stellar performance at his firm, he appears to be wildly inefficient with his shopping time. A tie one day ("Chris Caldwell looks very nice in paisley"), a shirt the next ("Chris Caldwell can wear those blue oxford shirts with the white collars and not look the least bit silly"). A black belt to go with his new English leather loafers ("He has such a trim 32-inch waist! Chris Caldwell always has been quite the athlete.").

Could you please tell me what in the hell has been going on in that store of yours? I mean, I'm sure people are respectful of your dad's memory and aren't in there flirting it up with your mother, but what is going on with MY mom? Maybe I should be happy for her to have "Chris Caldwell" lurking about, but I was pretty blindsided by the whole thing and would have appreciated a little heads-up.

And now to conclude my crazy week, I'm going to my last track team practice. All the injured runners are back so the team is at full strength, which means they don't need me anymore. I'm glad I trained with them, and I'm also kind of glad that it's over. It's a huge time and energy commitment. I've loved it, and I've learned so much from the coaches and made some really good friends—did I ever tell you about Donna and Donna-with-the-Headbands?—but I'm ready to go back to running on my own time. Plus they're letting me keep my team warm-up suit, which is awesome, and they know that I am really psyched for cross-country in the fall, which will be a better fit for me anyway. I'm all about long distances.

Okay, I'm off. Write soon, and don't forget that my birthday is coming up.

Say hi to the Moms for me, and keep an eye on that "Chris Caldwell" guy.

And congratulations again, college boy!

Love from your almost-nineteen-year-old friend who kissed you once in a bar, big deal,
Jennifer's sister,
Cath

P.S. It's baseball season already? Break out the pants, boys!

April 12, 1983

Cath,

I have no idea who "Chris Caldwell" is. Or at least I didn't until I got your letter. Now I'm figuring it must be that guy who comes in here who the Moms are always giggling about. Seems like a nice enough guy, but your mom literally has not said a word to me about him. She may have said something to Todd about him, since he's practically an honorary Mom at this point. In fact, if your mom ends up marrying the guy, I'd suspect that Todd would be one of the bridesmaids. Anyway, if I hear anything about it, I'll let you know.

I don't know what you're talking about when you say you only know a few of our songs. We have eight original songs right now, and I think you've heard all of them, although you might not have realized they were songs we'd written ourselves. I admit one of them sounds a lot like a Talking Heads song, and another sounds a lot like Squeeze, so maybe you didn't realize we'd stolen them—oops, I mean written them ourselves.

I did end up rewriting the lyrics to "Um." I liked the original version, but after we played it at a gig a week or so ago, a girl came up and told me she thought it was a great idea for a song, but that the lyrics sounded too "facile." I looked it up, and it means "simple." I have to admit she was right. Anyway, I've been re-working the lyrics in my head during downtime at the store to avoid listening to the Moms. Here are the current lyrics, although they may change again:

> I've been wasting my time for too many years,
> Watched too much TV, drank an ocean of beer,
> Woke up early and stayed up late,
> Though how early I got up is up for debate.
> I tell you I was lost, but now I'm found.
> 'Cause I bought this guitar and I like how it sounds.
>
> I graduated high school, if you can believe.
> My favorite class? How to underachieve.
> It might take me a second to recall who shot Lincoln.
> If I don't answer right away, it's not 'cause I'm not thinkin'.
> Because I'm not stupid, I'm not dumb.
> When I don't know what to say, I just say, "Um."
>
> Um, um, um.
> Um, um, um.
>
> I've heard it ever since I was a kid.
> How my brain didn't work like the other kids' did.
> "Maybe another school would be better instead."
> "Maybe his mother dropped him right on his head."
> But being different don't mean that I'm dumb.
> When I don't know what to say, I just say, "Um."

Um, um, um.
Um, um, um.

Now singing these songs don't pay my bills,
And if we don't cut a hit record, it never will.
So during the day I sell men's clothes. (Band: It's true!)
Ten hours a day, that totally blows.
Guy says his waist's 30 inches, give or take some.
Instead of saying, "Man, it's 36," I just say, "Um."

Um, um, um.
Um, um, um.

Now I'm not crazy about songs that turn into confessions,
I want three power chords, not Sunday school lessons.
But having said that, let me confess,
I almost dropped dead when you wore that red dress.
My other thoughts that night, well, I'd rather keep mum.
What did I say to you? I just said, "Um."

Um, um, um.
Um, um, um.

Yes, I had to go to school in the summers,
Think my grades were bad, you should've seen our drummer's.
Call us stupid? Here's my ass, you can kiss it.

But this song's not really about me, now, is it?
This song's about you, so just let me strum.
When I can't say I love you, I just say, "Um."

Um, um, um.
Um, um, um.

Remember the time you wore that bikini?
I'd give you a 10, that's more than Fellini. (Band: Who?)
That time we held hands when you were crying?
If I should have kissed you, it's my fault for not trying.
Add this all up and what is the sum?
All I have to say to you is, "Um."

Um, um, um.
Um, um, um.

Now everyone listening as I sing this song,
This is the part where you all sing along.
Sing so loud that the roof crumbles to powder,
Those in the back will just have to sing louder.
Clap your hands until they're numb.
If you want the boy to get the girl, just sing, "Um!"

Um, um, um.
Um, um, um.

If you want the boy to kiss the girl, just sing, "Um!"

If you think that maybe, just maybe, she might love him, too, sing, "Um!"

If you believe in the life-saving force of a love that is pure, just sing, "Um!"

If there's someone you love but you've never said it, just sing, "Um!"

If you're going to tell them today or tomorrow or next week, just sing, "Um!"

If you want the world to know how you feel, sing, "Um!"

Sing with me!
Um, um, um.
Um, um, um.

Let me know what you think of the new lyrics. I think it's a much better song now. Not as facile. We played it at a show the other night, and the crowd seemed to like it. Not as many people joined in at the sing-along part at the end as I would have liked, but that's okay. You can only expect so much from a crowd of drunks.

Scott

P.S. What's the deal with your family and ridiculous middle names? First, they give you the middle name "Fucking." Now your sister gets stuck with "Crystalle." It's definitely the name she should use if she ends up dancing at a club by the airport.

P.P.S. We'll hang out this summer. I promise. I've been thinking about some things lately that I want to talk with you about, but they can wait until you get home. Or at least I think they can.

April 15, 1983

Dear Scott:

The lyrics to "Um" are great. Despite what you may think, you've never played that song for me, so I have to imagine what it sounds like, and it sounds great in my head. And I hope Samantha likes it, too, and appreciates having a boyfriend who writes a song about her like that. Although, if you don't mind, can I offer a little friendly advice? If you're talking about the dress Samantha wore to the senior prom, it was a pink dress, not a red one. You might want to change that lyric fast. We hate it when our boyfriends don't pay enough attention to our hair or clothes.

Anyway, I'd really love to hear you sing the song, and I know your ever-expanding fan base here at Wake would love to hear it, too. Since your St. Patty's Day gig, I've had a lot of people comment on the Crush sticker on my backpack. I wish that you could come back to Wake and play one more time before exam reading period, particularly since you'll be off in college next year, but since you didn't mention it in your last letter, I'm guessing it's too much to ask, given the Samantha Factor and all.

Well, even if you and Crush refuse to serenade me, I will be having fun on my birthday! Jane, Steve (her boyfriend), some of my running friends (complete and utter lightweights), and my remaining Pizza Pan coworkers (heavyweight champions) are going out for drinks and dinner at the Carolina Ale House in Winston-Salem tomorrow night. I will let you know how it goes. You will note that

Andrew is not invited. That date ended up being a waste of a nice new dress, to put it mildly. Maybe I should have guessed that the conversation with an aerospace engineering major would have been a struggle, even if he does look like Rob Lowe.

I'm really glad to hear that you're going to be up for hanging out some this summer. I'm going to need at least one constant in my life. I mean, my dad lives with his secretary in another town, I have a baby sister, and my mom is running on about some dude she knew in high school a hundred years ago when she's not gabbing with your mom and my old boyfriend at your store. It's going to take some getting used to.

Please tell Todd and the Moms that they should drink a lot of milk during menopause, to prevent brittle bones.

Much love,
Cath

P.S. We got our housing assignments for next year, and Jane and I got a double in our first-choice dorm! Dorothy got a single, so she and James can go on basically living together. I'm happy for them.

P.P.S. Curious to know what you have to wait until the summer to talk to me about. How embarrassing could it be? A bad case of acne? Whatever it is, come on, tell me!

April 20, 1983

Cath,

As much as I'd like to come down to Wake to play another gig during reading period, I can't. Putting Samantha aside, things are so busy here at work, particularly since I have to train the Moms and Todd on how to run the store once I go off to college, and we've got gigs lined up every weekend for the next couple months.

Also, I know Samantha wore a pink dress to our prom. I mean, I was there. But "red dress" sounds better.

My mom has been acting very strange ever since I got accepted to college. Keep in mind that it was her idea to call all those colleges to see if they'd let me apply late. Now that I actually got into one, she's been very sad. You don't need to be a genius to figure it out. A few months ago, she had her husband and her son living with her. In a couple months, she'll be living by herself. I've already told her that I'm going to try to come back as many weekends as I can—which also will allow me to keep playing with Crush—but I don't know if that will be enough. I'm thinking I should get her a dog before I leave. And I'm really glad that she and your mom have become such good friends.

Good luck with your exams!

Scott

April 24, 1983

Dear Scott,

I'm sorry you won't be able to get down here to play a gig. I guess I'll just have to focus on exams and look forward to seeing you when I get home when you can tell me whatever you can't tell me now. Can't you at least tell me what it rhymes with?

I'm glad our moms have become good friends, too. The thought of the two of them co-managing Agee's Men's Clothing without you makes me smile. That place could look considerably different by the time you get home for Thanksgiving break. I'm imagining a lot of cat posters on the wall and doilies on the countertops! Seriously, though, they'll do a great job. I mean, look at the job they did with us. Or, at least, one of us.

By the way, I've been swapping letters with Todd since the incident at Christmas. They're a lot different from your letters and, believe it or not, contain even more spelling errors. (Sorry, but I had to say that. Todd couldn't spell "cat" if you spotted him the *C* and the *A*.) Without telling you everything he has to say, please know that he is very grateful to you and your family. He loves working at the store and being in the band with you, and he's going to miss you when you go off to college. I mention that to you only because I want you to be gentle with him if he acts strange in the weeks before you leave for college. Acting strange before someone you care about goes off to college . . . Seems unimaginable, doesn't it?

I feel like I'm going to be completely prepared for my finals this semester. I'm not saying I'm going to ace them all, but I've done a pretty good job of keeping up with my work throughout the semester, and I should feel prepared and comfortable after the reading period. And if I do get straight A's, you're going to have to buy me a cake that says "Congratulations, Straight-A Girl!" or whatever it said on that cake Dorothy's parents got her.

Amanda keeps sending new pictures of Jennifer. She's absolutely, completely adorable. (Jennifer, not Amanda.) Of course, that shouldn't be a surprise. My family churns out adorable girls, in case you haven't noticed.

Okay, I'm going off for a long run with Donna-with-the-Headbands before moving into my library cubicle for the next few weeks.

Love,
Cath

April 27, 1983

Dear Cath,

I have some news, and I'm not sure how you're going to feel about it. I probably should wait until after you're done with your finals, but if I don't tell you now, your mom will. And although I made your mom swear she wouldn't say anything, I'm not sure how long I should trust that. So my news is that I got a letter in the mail from a college I'd been wait-listed for. They let me know that they now have a slot for me and they hope I'll start school there in the fall. I have to tell you that it really surprised me. It's a much, much better school than Samantha's, and I didn't think there was any way they would ever let me in. They have a great English department and a pretty good music department, too, and their reputation should help me get a good job almost anywhere in the country. But, of course, Samantha isn't there.

I almost wish I hadn't gotten in off the wait list, because my decision was so easy before. Not that there really was a decision before. If you get into only one college, that's the college you go to. So I talked about it with my mom. My mom likes Samantha, but her point was that this is my only chance to go to college, and shouldn't I go to the best one instead of making a decision based on who I'm dating? What if I go to school with Samantha, and we break up again? What if she does something to hurt me again, like she did at Thanksgiving (which my mom apparently knows all about, and so did my dad)? Wouldn't I regret not going to the other school, the better one? And if I did go to the other school, couldn't I still date Samantha long-distance?

I tried to tell her how I felt about Samantha, and how my dad always liked her and thought we would get married some-day. And she said my dad would've liked anyone I liked, and that he said the same thing about me getting married to every girl I've ever dated. And I thought about that, and it was true. Every girl I've ever dated since I was in third grade, he made the exact same comment: "Look, it's Mr. and Mrs. Scott Agee." He just said it more about Samantha than the others because I dated her longer.

She said the only girl he never made that joke about was you. When I said that it was because you and I never dated, she said that it was because my dad knew better than to make a joke about me and you.

Anyway, I've been thinking about everything my mom said, and she's 100% right. I should go to the best college I get into.

So, I'm not going to college with Samantha this fall. Instead, I'm going to college with . . . you.

Yes, I got into Wake Forest. Which I believe is located in North Dakota.

Cath, I know I should have told you before that I'd applied there, but I didn't want you to feel bad if I didn't get in. And I really didn't think I would get in. But I did. And I have a letter to prove it on official Wake Forest stationery with a seal and everything. Unlike the fake Wake Forest stationery you got in the school bookstore.

So, unless I get something in the mail telling me it was a mistake, I'll be seeing you a lot the next few years.

I hope you're okay with that.

Scott

April 30, 1983

Dear Scott,

Okay with it?

Okay with it?

Okay with going to college with you?

Okay with hanging out with you in person and talking like we did when we were Tornadoes instead of writing a letter and having to wait DAYS for a response?

Okay with it?

I wish I could write more, but I have an Abnormal Psych review session in 5 minutes, so let me just say this—

Am I okay with it? Hell yeah! I'll be the happiest girl in the world!

Love,
Cath

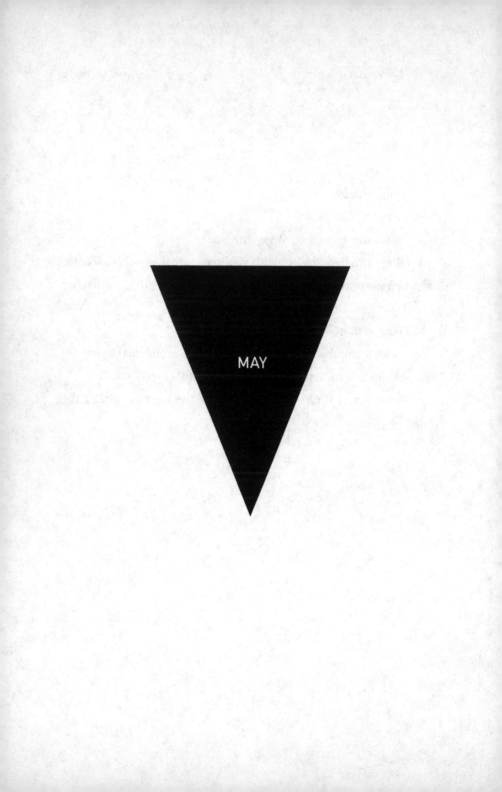

May 4, 1983

Cath—

Me, too!

Scott

May 4, 1983

Cath—

I mean, the happiest guy. Not the happiest girl.

   Scott

P.S. I hope you didn't throw away any of your Biology notes from first semester. I may need them next year. Actually, don't throw out any of your notes from any of your classes, okay?

May 7, 1983

Scott—

I knew what you meant. I always know what you mean.

And I wasn't going to throw out any of my notes, so they're all yours. Although there are a few months in there where my notetaking wasn't particularly focused, for reasons you are well aware of, so you are relying upon them at your own risk.

I shouldn't even ask, but have you told Samantha yet that you're going to Wake next year? I can't imagine she's going to be too happy. I mean, first you write a song about how you have trouble telling her you love her, then you have to tell her you're not going to go to college with her? Good luck with *that*. I can hear the cursing from here.

By the way, you know that sophomore girls don't hang out with freshman boys at Wake, right? It would be a social faux pas of biblical proportions. So I'll be ignoring you when anyone else is around!

Love,
Cath

P.S. Finals start on Monday. I have three exams and one Poetry paper to crank out, and then, about two weeks from now, my first year of college will be done and I will officially be a sophomore!

P.P.S. Just kidding about the social faux pas thing. Or so you hope!

May 10, 1983

Dear Cath,

I guess I'll just have to hang out with the junior girls, then! They seemed more mature anyway.

As for how Samantha took the news, let's just say it didn't go over very well. And that would be an understatement. In case you're wondering, I'm a "pathetic loser" and a "fucking piece of shit" who "led her on" and "wasted her fucking time" when there were plenty of other "better looking" guys who would "walk over a pile of shit on fire" just to be with her. (How's that for overusing quotation marks?) So she broke up with me. Again. And I can't even pretend that it hurt this time, because it didn't. This may sound terrible, but it kind of felt like a relief. I think I've known it wasn't right since I visited her, but it was hard to admit that when I thought I might be going to school with her.

So that's over. I actually had a harder time when I told the band that I'm leaving at the end of the summer. And they were considerably cooler about it than Samantha was. No one called me a "fucking piece of shit."

Now I have to get back to work. Not only do we have to put all the summer clothes out, but I need to teach the Moms how to reconcile the books and how to calculate the withholdings on their paychecks. And I have to order some more stationery for the store because somehow most of it disappeared this year. Do you have any idea how expensive stationery is? It's not cheap.

Good luck with your next final, college girl.

Scott

P.S. I had to look up "faux pas." If you'd just written "fo pa," I would've gotten it.

P.P.S. And whoever said I wrote "Um" about Samantha anyway? I never had trouble saying "I love you" to Samantha, even though I'm not sure I meant it. Maybe I wrote that song about someone else.

WAKE FOREST
UNIVERSITY

May 13, 1983

Scott—

WHAT?
Who?

Cath

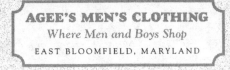

AGEE'S MEN'S CLOTHING
Where Men and Boys Shop
EAST BLOOMFIELD, MARYLAND

May 15, 1983

Dear Cath,

Think, college girl. Use that big brain of yours. Who wore a red dress to our senior prom?

If you can't figure it out, we can talk about it when you get home.

Scott

May 18, 1983

Scott—

Well, Nancy Gilmartin wore that low-cut red minidress. Linda Hes-
ter wore that red one with the white collar. The only other girl who
wore a red dress was me. I wore that red one with the spaghetti
straps that you teased me about. Remember how you kept saying the
straps didn't look strong enough and you kept threatening to cut
them? Funny, very funny.

Hold on.

Wait a second.

Wait another second. I haven't gotten very much sleep lately
because of exams, but . . . me? Do you mean me?

Cath

May 20, 1983

Dear Cath,

Um, yeah, you. I was going to tell you when you got home. Or sing it to you.

Great dress, by the way. Very red.

Scott

WAKE FOREST
UNIVERSITY

May 22, 1983

Scott—

Well, um, right back at you, college boy.

Right back at you.

Now, if you don't mind, I'm having trouble breathing for obvious reasons, and I have to run to turn in my Poetry paper before 5 p.m.

I'll swing by the post office on my way. I may get home before this letter does. I can't wait to see you!

Much love,
Cath

JUNE

I'm so happy we're in the same place again.
And I meant what I said last night.

I love you, too.

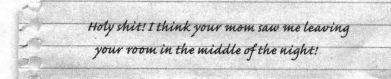

Holy shit! I think your mom saw me leaving your room in the middle of the night!

Holy shit, who cares!

JULY

Happy Fourth of July, sweetie!

I think you left these in my room. They don't look like mine. Although I would look pretty good in them.

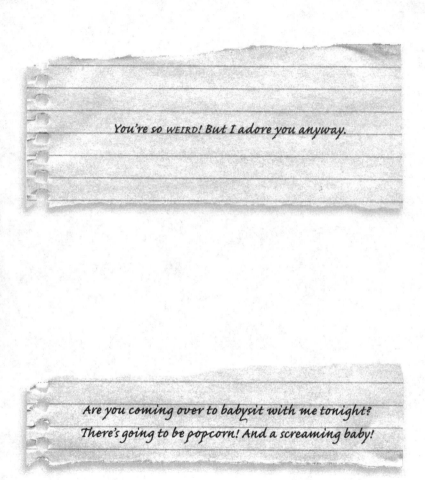

You're so WEIRD! But I adore you anyway.

Are you coming over to babysit with me tonight?
There's going to be popcorn! And a screaming baby!

AUGUST

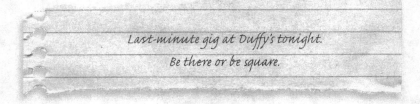

Last-minute gig at Duffy's tonight.
Be there or be square.

Tell the lead singer I'm crazy about him.

Tell that girl in the audience that I know.

Two weeks to college! Yippee!

Thank you for the best summer in the history of summers!

WAKE FOREST
UNIVERSITY

August 27, 1983

Dear Scott—

Welcome to college, freshman!

> Love you,
> *Cath*

P.S. Nice underwear. I warned you that college guys wear boxers. I told you a million times. When you're the only guy in your dorm sitting around in tighty-whities, don't come running to me.

P.P.S. Okay, you can come running to me.

P.P.P.S. You can always come running to me.

ACKNOWLEDGMENTS

From Susan

I'd like to thank my husband, Kevin, and our daughters, Haley and Hannah, for reading early drafts of the manuscript and providing great feedback and loving support throughout this project. You guys are my rock and I wouldn't have the strength to venture forth into this new world without you.

I'd also like to thank my sister Liz Sesemann, my sister and brother-in-law Kada and Jay Jedlicka, as well as my father, John Stevens, my stepsister Cathy Silver, my dear friends Jennie Treeger Bowen, Mary Donald Mehigan, Gary Lisker, and my Cooley LLP friends Erin Ramana, Jack Lavoie, Tony Calabrese, and Michelle Schulman, among others, for their kindness and enthusiastic support of this book.

Special thanks to our agent, Steven Axelrod, and our editor, Rose Hilliard, for their excellent and professional guidance and help.

And importantly, I'd like to thank my coauthor, Michael Kun, for asking me to write this book with him; for his kindness, patience, support, and friendship; and for bringing out the writer in me.

From Michael

There are many people whose kindness and support contributed to this book. I start, of course, with thanks to my wife, Amy, and our daughter, Paige. Amy read early drafts of the book and provided just the right amount of encouragement, and in addition to being understanding when I was typing while she was trying to sleep, Paige supplied the name of the dog in the book, which she would like me to acknowledge here. And I just did.

Thanks to my mother, Beatrice Kun.

Thanks to our editor, Rose Hilliard, for her enthusiasm and guidance, and our agent, Steven Axelrod, for putting the book in her hands. It's been an absolute pleasure working with such a talented and generous editor. And if any readers have a problem with the fact that some occasional foul language has snuck through the final draft of the book, kindly send your complaints to Rose in care of this publisher. I'll just throw your complaints out if you send them to me.

Special thanks to my longtime friends Dave and Carol Weymer, who provided valuable assistance with matters relating to their alma mater, Wake Forest University, which plays a prominent role in the book.

Thanks to friends who read early drafts of this book and shared their thoughts, especially Pete and Beth Johnson, Michael Callahan, Bill Stein, Theresa Hoiles, Gary Campbell, Andy Bienstock, Howard Cohen, Arlene Lynes, Sandra Siciliano, Brent Houk, and Stan Smith.

I would be remiss if I didn't take this opportunity to thank my former writing professor at Johns Hopkins, Stephen Dixon. I simply cannot say often enough that I would never have written or published a word had our paths not crossed many, many years ago.

And I can say the same thing about my coauthor, Susan Mullen, who encouraged me to start writing again after I had given it up to attend law school. I thank her for that and for working with me on this fun and unusual project. It has been a pleasure. There is no other writer who I could have written this with, let alone one who could do it with as much joy, patience, and tolerance.